"I'm afraid this isn't going to work out."

Gemma stared at Nate. "You can't be serious?"

His blue eyes glinted. "I've never been more serious."

She threw out her hands. "But why?"

He lifted his Stetson off his head and placed it again on top of his short, dark hair. "I think you know why."

"That was a long time ago." She raised her chin. "The program would be a godsend for your father. Having a dementia service dog companion could potentially extend his independence several years beyond what most patients with his condition experience. Rascal will also help you shoulder some of the day-to-day burden of caring for him. Your wife, too."

His ruggedly handsome features creased. "My wife is dead. It's only me, the boys and Dad."

She reared a fraction. She hadn't realized he was a widower. She'd assumed... Wrongly as it turned out.

"I'm sorry." She bit her lip. "I didn't know."

"How could you know? I haven't heard a word from you in fifteen years."

Lisa Carter and her family make their home in North Carolina. In addition to her Love Inspired novels, she writes romantic suspense. When she isn't writing, Lisa enjoys traveling to romantic locales, teaching writing workshops and researching her next exotic adventure. She has strong opinions on barbecue and ACC basketball. She loves to hear from readers. Connect with Lisa at lisacarterauthor.com.

Books by Lisa Carter

Love Inspired

K-9 Companions

Visit the Author Profile page at LoveInspired.com for more titles.

A K-9 Christmas Reunion

LISA CARTER

LOVE INSPIRED
INSPIRATIONAL ROMANCE

LOVE INSPIRED®
INSPIRATIONAL ROMANCE

ISBN-13: 978-1-335-93678-3

A K-9 Christmas Reunion

Copyright © 2024 by Lisa Carter

Love Inspired
22 Adelaide St. West, 41st Floor
Toronto, Ontario M5H 4E3, Canada
www.LoveInspired.com

Printed in Lithuania

Recycling programs for this product may not exist in your area.

MIX
Paper | Supporting responsible forestry
FSC® C021394

For I know the thoughts that I think toward you,
saith the Lord, thoughts of peace, and not of evil,
to give you an expected end.
—*Jeremiah* 29:11

To Leslie-Jean—thank you for praying me through.

Chapter One

Running behind schedule had become the story of Nate Crenshaw's life.

From the start, his day—like most of his days since his wife died two years ago—had gone heels over head. First, he discovered the downed section of fence. The cattle had escaped from the grazing pasture into his neighbor's property.

He spent the morning rounding up the cattle into a temporary holding pen, but he didn't have enough materials to properly secure the breach in the fence. Which meant driving into town to acquire the necessary wire from the agri-supply store.

With each tick of the clock, today's to-do list faded further out of reach. Tires kicking up a cloud of dust, he steered around the bend of trees on the graveled drive of the High Country Ranch. Barreling under the crossbars, he took the secondary road leading over the mountain to his hometown of Truelove, North Carolina.

The blistering heat of summer had long since given way to the crisp coolness of mid-November. The blaze of autumn color, for which the Blue Ridge was famous, now carpeted the forest floor. The hardwood trees lifted stark, bare branches to the Carolina blue sky.

With his father having one of his good days, when Nate returned with his supplies, he didn't stop to check on his dad. He gathered his tools from the barn and headed to the pasture on the far edge of the ranch to make the repairs. He'd have to hurry to make the appointment the agency had set up for him and his dad.

It was important the meeting go well. Their future depended on how well his father took to the new, specially trained dementia service dog. As soon as his dad had gotten his diagnosis, Nate had put him on the list to receive a dog. They'd waited almost eighteen months for this day to arrive.

With his father in the early stages of the disease, this was the optimal time to pair him with a service animal. Nate had high hopes the dog trained by Juliet Melbourne's canine agency, PawPals, would make a real difference in alleviating some of the worst symptoms of his dad's heartbreaking and progressive illness.

Clearing his mind of everything else, Nate got to work. By the time he finished, his head was pounding. He probably shouldn't have skipped lunch. When he looked up from the wire he'd strung, the sun sat much lower on the horizon. The repairs had taken longer than he'd anticipated.

He took a deep breath of the tangy scent of evergreens lining the perimeter of the pasture. He loved ranching. He'd never wanted to live anywhere else or do anything else.

Not exactly true. He frowned. There'd been a brief time, long ago, when he'd believed he wanted something quite different in a place far from here.

A temporary insanity from which life—and a particular girl—had soon disabused him. This was his life now, and he loved it. Except when the loneliness got to him.

Bone weary, he put his tools and what was left of the wire roll into the back of his pickup. He climbed behind the wheel. Scrubbing his forehead, he willed the headache to subside. These days, he stayed tired. It had been a while since Dad had been able to help on the farm.

Cranking the engine, Nate jostled down the rutted path toward the barn. The boys would be wondering where he was. He liked to be there when they got home from school. Yet despite how hard he tried, he'd failed them once again.

Not for the first time, he thought how much better Deanna would have coped as a single parent. But she was the one who died, and he was the one left to pick up the pieces of an unimaginable future spent without her.

Holding the leash of a medium-sized, sable-colored rough collie, a woman with indistinct features emerged from the shadows cast by the barn.

Gut churning, he suddenly realized he was late for the appointment with the trainer from PawPals. He braked sharply, sending gravel spinning. The woman jerked.

Nate threw himself out of the vehicle. *Way to make a terrible first impression, Crenshaw.*

He hoped his dad had stepped into the gap due to his lack of hospitality. The boys had been looking forward to the dog coming to live with them. Probably lively five-year-old Kody and seven-year-old Connor had more than made up for his absence and provided a most cordial welcome.

From a distance, his first impressions of the dog trainer were of her even, pleasing features. She was pretty in an outdoorsy way. Compared to his six-foot height, she wasn't tall. Maybe only five foot five. Casually dressed in jeans, brown ankle boots and an oversize beige sweater, she wore her hair in a pale golden braid, which hung over her shoulder.

Tromping across the yard to meet her, he raised his hand. The dog yipped a greeting. "I'm so sorry I'm late, Ms. Spencer. I meant to be here to greet you, but the time got away from me."

She stepped out of the shadows and into the slanted light of the sun. A slight breeze fluttered the blue silk ribbon tied around the end of her braid. Once upon a lifetime ago, he'd known a girl who wore her hair the same way.

Hand outstretched, he got his first glimpse of her face. A face that teased at the edges of his memory. "Welcome to—"

The pieces of an all-too-familiar puzzle clicked into place. His heart skipping a beat, he came to a complete halt.

"Gemma?" He blinked at her. "Gemma Anderson?" Dropping his hand, he went rigid. "You're the dog trainer Juliet sent?"

She stiffened. "It's Spencer now. And yes, I'm here to help your father bond with Rascal."

He flicked a look at the collie sitting quietly at her feet. "Rascal?"

The dog cocked his head.

She flipped the end of her braid over her shoulder. "It suited him in an entirely endearing way."

He folded his arms across his chest. "I'm sorry you came all this way for nothing. This isn't going to work out."

Gemma's heart skipped a beat. "You can't be serious?"

Rascal rubbed his nose against her hand. The collie always sensed when his humans needed emotional support. It was this sensitivity that made him such a great service dog.

Nathan's blue eyes glinted. "I've never been more serious."

She threw out her hands. "But why?"

He lifted his Stetson off his head and placed it again on top of his short, dark hair. "I think you know why."

As seventeen-year-olds, they'd met as 4-H camp counselors. During that unforgettable summer, they fell in love.

"I wasn't sure you'd remember me," she rasped.

When the summer ended, they vowed to love each other forever. But after she returned to her home near Greensboro in the Piedmont, her world fell apart.

She immediately ended her budding relationship with him, stopped answering his letters and refused to take his phone calls. Later, she'd heard through the 4-H grapevine, he and a former girlfriend got married.

"No one ever forgets their first love." He threw her a piercing look. "Nor the Dear John left in my voicemail the very next day."

Because the next day after she returned home, her mother was dead and her father in prison. The shame had been too much. Recalling that terrible day brought only darkness. A downward spiral into an abyss she'd barely managed to survive.

She couldn't—wouldn't—go back to that time in her life. Better for him to believe her coldhearted than to ever learn the truth. With an effort, she steadied her rioting emotions.

"That was a long time ago. Today I'm here to help your dad." She raised her chin. "The program would be a godsend for your father. A dementia service dog could potentially extend his independence several years beyond what most patients with his condition experience. Rascal will also help you and your wife shoulder the day-to-day burden of caring for him."

His ruggedly handsome features creased. "My wife is dead. It's only me, the boys and Dad."

She reared a fraction. She hadn't realized he was a widower. She'd assumed… Wrongly as it turned out.

"I'm sorry." She bit her lip. "I didn't know."

"How could you know?" He peered at the evergreen-studded mountain range that enfolded the ranch like the worn but comforting arms of a beloved grandmother. "I haven't heard from you in fifteen years." His gaze locked onto hers.

She flushed. "There were reasons…"

His eyebrow arched.

She could feel the heat creeping up her neck. "Reasons I'd rather not discuss."

Nathan's lips—such a handsome mouth—tightened. "Look, I don't want to cause problems for you with your boss. I'll tell Juliet we weren't a good fit. And request a different trainer to acclimate my father to Rascal."

Hearing his name, the collie woofed.

For a split second, Nathan's tense features relaxed. A tentative smile lurked at the corners of his lips. Like her, he'd always loved dogs, but too soon a weight settled upon his countenance once more.

Her heart fluttered against her rib cage at the brief glimpse of the warm-hearted teenager she'd loved so deeply. Judging from his broad shoulders, Nathan the man had fulfilled the physical potential of the adolescent she'd known. Otherwise, probably little remained of the boy she recalled. Little enough remained of the girl she'd been.

Life had a way of doing that. After their glorious summer together, she'd had to grow up fast. But Gemma wasn't ready to give up on the PawPals program, which she and her best friend, Juliet, had piloted.

"I'm afraid it doesn't work that way." She glanced at her dog. "Stay." Dropping the leash, she moved closer to the thirty-two-year-old rancher.

"There are only a few facilities in the nation that train dementia assistance canines. And there are even less trainers than there are dogs. Without me, there can be no service dog for your father. He'll lose his place on the waiting list to another family in desperate need of help." She pursed her lips. "By the time another dog and trainer become available—"

"Another eighteen months?"

She nodded. "Possibly two years. At which point, your father might no longer benefit from the program."

A bleakness clouded his gaze. "You mean he could have slipped too far from us?"

Her heart pinged inside her chest. "Dementia companion dogs typically make the biggest difference with patients in the early- to mid- stages of dementia. After that…" She sighed. "I'm sorry."

"You and Rascal are a package deal." He scoured his face with his hand. "Got it."

"The training only lasts a few weeks. Just until your father is comfortable with Rascal. Just until I'm sure Rascal has bonded to him, and we establish a routine."

"What kind of routine?"

She smiled. "You'll be amazed at what Rascal can do for your father, once I identify what would be of most help to your dad. In the application, you mentioned sundowner events. Late in the day confusion and sleep issues are fairly typical of a patient with your father's illness. Once attuned to your dad, Rascal will be able to reduce the severity of the agitation your father experiences and sometimes divert an episode altogether."

He pinched the bridge of his nose. "Those episodes are the worst. Upsetting not only for my dad, but the boys, too. They don't understand why their granddad suddenly…" His Adam's apple bobbed in his throat.

She put her hand on the sleeve of his tan Carhartt jacket. "If you'll give me the chance to work with your father, I believe Rascal could enrich all your lives."

He searched her face.

Not entirely sure why this mattered so much, she held her breath. There were lots of other families in need of Rascal's services. If he sent her away, she and Rascal would become a blessing to someone else.

She tilted her head. "Surely you can put up with me for two weeks?"

For a second, something she couldn't decipher flitted across his features. A muscle ticked in his square-lined jaw. She let go of his arm. Touching him had been a mistake.

She prided herself on her professionalism, but Nathan Crenshaw was far from being just another client. For a multitude of reasons, she'd sensed seeing him would be hard, and she'd steeled herself for the upcoming training. Yet being with him again… The intensity of feeling was far more than she'd anticipated.

Rattled, she preferred not to examine too closely why she so badly wanted this to work out for him. She wanted the dogs she trained to work out for every family. What she was feeling was probably nothing more than the emotional equivalent of an aftershock. What else could it be?

"My father's happiness and well-being are the only things that matter." He touched a finger to the brim of his hat. "We'll give it a try."

A shaft of sheer joy pierced her heart.

She threw Nate a dazzling smile. "You won't be sorry."

Bits of the Gemma he'd fallen in love with that long ago summer sparkled in her soft brown eyes.

To his ultimate heartbreak, he'd discovered she wasn't the girl he'd believed her to be. But according to the credentials Juliet Melbourne forwarded, prior to specializing in the training and placement of dementia service dogs, Gemma Spencer had an extensive résumé of working with patients in memory-care facilities. The program at PawPals provided families an at-home care option for their loved ones.

He didn't delude himself about what his father's future would hold. Nate had done his research. Diagnosed in his late sixties, his dad could live for many more years.

The progressive disease, this most terrible of illnesses, would eventually rob Ike Crenshaw of everything that made him who he was. If his dad lived long enough, one day permanent placement in a care facility would become a necessary reality.

But if Rascal could truly improve his father's quality of life… Nate would be a fool to turn down this opportunity.

His sons had already lost so much. He needed to do everything in his power to ensure their granddad was there for them—in every sense of the word—for as long as possible.

Nate wasn't a lovesick teenager anymore. He was an adult. A son and a father in his own right. A privilege and a responsibility he didn't take lightly.

He'd find a way to work with Gemma. Yet forewarned was forearmed. She'd proved she couldn't be trusted. It would be best to keep her at arm's length.

Leash in hand, she walked the service dog forward. "Rascal, meet Nathan. Nathan, this is Rascal."

Something bittersweet pinged inside his chest. He'd forgotten she always used his full given name. She was the only one who ever had.

Rascal lifted a paw and placed it atop Nate's hand.

"Go ahead. Shake his paw. He's waiting for you." She smiled at him in such a winsome way, for a moment his earlier resolve wavered.

Arm's length might prove easier said than done. He gave the collie's paw a tentative shake. Rascal dropped his paw to the ground, and brushed his head against Nate's leg.

"If you rub the spot below his ears, he'll love you fur-ever." She winked. "Get it? Fur-ever?"

Despite his intention to remain aloof, his lips twitched. He'd also forgotten how she used to make him laugh. Usually at the lamest, silliest things.

It was reassuring to know something of the girl he'd once fallen for so hard still remained in the coolly sophisticated woman standing in front of him.

He stroked the dog's fluffy fur. "It's great to finally meet you, Rascal."

The collie licked his hand.

He smiled. "Rascal seems like an extraordinary dog. I'm surprised you're willing to let him go."

"Rascal is special. And believe me, I've trained a lot of service dogs over the years." Her smile became strained. "But it's because of his specialness I'm able to let go. Rascal will make such a significant difference to your family."

Nate stuffed his hands in his coat pockets. "How did Dad respond to Rascal?"

Her forehead puckered. "What do you mean?"

"Earlier, when Dad and the boys met Rascal."

She shook her head. "When we arrived, nobody answered the door. That's why we were in the barn looking for you."

"Nobody's home?" He stared at her. "That can't be right. I don't understand."

His eyes drifted to the sprawling white clapboard farmhouse. But the home he shared with his father and sons lay dark and shuttered. He glanced at his wristwatch. Five o'clock.

She wrapped the leash around her hand. "What's wrong?"

"Where's my dad?" A sick feeling coiled in his gut. "By now, the boys should've been home from school, too."

Like every other afternoon since school started in September, his second cousin Maggie brought his sons home when she picked up her own children. Where were Connor and Kody?

His gaze darted to the sky, swathed in swirls of golden pinks and apricots. But there was no time to appreciate the sunset. Once the sun slid below the ridge on the horizon, darkness would descend rapidly.

Breathing heavily, he dug his phone out of his jean pocket. His eyes widened.

While mending the fence in the back pasture, he'd missed a half-dozen phone calls. In rural areas outside town, cell reception was notoriously spotty.

Chest heaving, he scrolled through the calls. The school had called four times. Maggie had left three messages for him to call back ASAP.

What had happened? What was going on? Panicked, he hit Redial on the school number. Had there been an accident at school? Had his father taken the call and gone to the hospital to be with them?

His call to the school went unanswered. Everyone must have gone home for the evening. Frustrated, he disconnected.

"Would your dad have left a note?"

Cell pressed to his ear, he hurried toward the house. She kept pace with him. Rascal loped alongside.

Beyond the curve in the drive around the cluster of trees, he heard the sound of an engine.

Nate released the breath he hadn't realized he'd been holding. "Finally."

His relief was short-lived.

It wasn't Maggie's hunter green Outback or his dad's bronze GMC. Instead, a white cruiser, belonging to Truelove's chief of police, rounded the bend.

Fear robbing the oxygen from his lungs, Nate raced forward.

Chapter Two

Jumping out of the police cruiser, his cousin Maggie intercepted him a few feet from the vehicle. "Everything's okay, Nate."

He craned his neck, trying to get a better look at the occupants inside. "Where are my sons?"

"They're in the car with Bridger."

"I want to see them." He tried to step around her, but she held his arm in a firm grip.

"Let me explain before they get out."

"What's happened, Mags? When I realized you'd called so many times and the boys weren't home yet—"

"Bridger's got everything under control." The slim brunette squeezed his arm. "But the state you're in, you'll spook the boys again."

He cut a look over her shoulder at the police·chief—also her husband—sitting behind the wheel. The law enforcement officer gave him a small nod.

Nate's eyebrow arched. "What do you mean 'spook' them again?"

"There was an incident at school this afternoon."

His mouth went dry. "A shooter? In Truelove?"

"Not that." She shook her head. Her ponytail whipped back and forth. "Your dad showed up at the school office to collect the boys."

He frowned. "But Dad knows you take them home from school."

"Ike had it in his mind he was taking them home today." Her bottom lip wobbled. "He became agitated when Principal Stallings refused to call them out of their classrooms. Ike's name wasn't listed on the consent-to-release paperwork. By law, the school cannot relinquish physical custody of a child to a nonauthorized adult."

Nate slumped. "His name used to be on the form. This school year, out of concern for the boys, he agreed it would be better for you to take over carpool duties. Why would he take it into his head to do this?"

"Ike couldn't be reasoned with, Nate." Her brown eyes watered. "When the situation escalated, Mrs. Stallings phoned Bridger at the police station. I was already en route to the carpool line."

Nate scrubbed his hand over his face. "I'm so sorry you got dragged into the nightmare that has become our lives." He lifted his head. "Are Austin and Logan with you?"

Her twins were a year younger than Connor.

"Bridger's mom took the boys to her house. But what happened at school is not the worst of it, Nate." Her voice hitched.

Dread dropped like a stone into the pit of his stomach. "It gets worse?"

"Before Bridger could arrive, Ike grabbed Connor and Kody off the playground. They were scared, but they went with him because—"

"Because he's their grandfather and they love him." Nate rubbed his forehead. "Was there a car accident? Is my father dead, Mags?"

"Ike is shaken but all right. He became disoriented and couldn't find his way home. He'd been driving around for thirty minutes before Bridger and his deputies were able to locate the SUV."

"Dad's been okay driving to Truelove to see his buddies, or I never would have let him keep the keys to his car."

At the image of his dad driving erratically on the winding mountain roads surrounding Truelove with his precious sons in tow, Nate's heart plummeted.

"Anything could have happened, Mags. They could have plunged over the edge into the gorge," he whispered.

"But they didn't." She gave him a fierce hug. "God watched over them."

He jerked his chin at the police cruiser. "Is my dad in the car, too?"

She dropped her gaze. "Bridger believed it might be best if my father drove him home in Ike's SUV. We'll give Dad a lift back to his house when we pick up Austin and Logan."

Nate's dad and his first cousin Tom Arledge, Maggie's father, had been best friends since they were children.

"Dad and Ike should be here in a few minutes." She looked at him. "I wanted to give you a heads-up and the chance to speak to the boys before they arrived."

He swallowed past the lump in his throat. "I can't thank you and Bridger enough for what you did today for my family."

"We're family, too, cuz." She swiped a finger under her eyes. "We love you guys."

Taking a deep breath, he opened the back door. "Connor? Kody?"

Strapped into the seat, five-year-old Kody reached for him. "Daddy?" His small, forlorn face bore the unmistakable signs of tears.

Beside his brother, seven-year-old Connor's lower lip trembled. "I... I took care of Kody, Daddy. I made sure he was okay. But Granddad got lost." The child's face crumpled. "Why couldn't he find his way home? We tried to help him, but he wouldn't listen to us."

His heart broke. "You've been very brave, but it's my job

to take care of Kody and you. I'm sorry I wasn't there when you needed me."

Leaning in, he released Kody's seat belt and opened his arms. Both boys flew into his embrace. He gave them a tight hug. "I'm so sorry this happened, guys."

He helped them out of the car.

Kody tugged at his arm. "Is that our new doggie?"

Standing near the porch holding Rascal's leash, Gemma smiled at his sons.

"Hi." Striding forward, Maggie stuck out her hand. "I'm Nate's cousin, Maggie Hollingsworth." She motioned. "This is my husband, Bridger."

The police chief tipped the brim of his regulation hat to Gemma. "Ma'am."

Maggie cocked her head. "You must be the dog trainer lady. Ms. Spencer, right?"

"I am." She smiled. "Please call me Gemma."

"What a lovely name." Maggie flashed her eyes at him. "An unusual name I recollect only hearing once a long time ago."

He toed the dirt with his boot. "Mags…" he warned.

The collie barked.

"And this is Rascal." Gemma waggled her fingers at the boys. "That's his way of saying hello."

Connor stuck his thumbs into his belt loops. "Kind of a silly name for a dog."

She grinned. "Rascal can be a silly kind of dog. When he's not working, though, he loves nothing better than hanging out with silly boys. You wouldn't happen to know any silly boys, would you?"

Kody thrust his hand into the air. "Me! Sometimes I'm a silly boy."

Nate ruffled his hair. "Just sometimes?"

Connor took a cautious step forward. "Is Rascal working

now? Daddy said we mustn't pet Rascal if he's working with Granddad."

"Thank you for asking first." She led Rascal forward. "I'm so happy your dad explained the service dog rules. Rascal's off duty until your grandfather gets here. He would love to get to know you better. It's okay to pet him if you want."

The boys looked at him. He nodded. Gemma showed them where Rascal liked to be petted.

Connor stroked the dog's head. "You have to be gentle, Kody," he admonished his younger brother.

Not unlike Nate, the second-grader had an overly developed sense of responsibility. Since Deanna died, Connor had taken it upon himself to act as a surrogate parent to his kid brother. It pained Nate that his too-serious firstborn had borne the brunt of taking care of Kody. Connor deserved to be a kid, too.

Kody gave the collie a pat. Rascal licked his hand. The kindergartener's blue eyes widened. "He licked me, Miss Gemma."

"That means he likes you."

Giggling, Kody put his hand over his mouth. "I love Wascal."

Nate jammed his hands in his pockets. "Kody sometimes has trouble with his *r*'s."

She winked at his son. "Don't we all?"

His lips quirked. This was exactly how he remembered her dealing with the young campers in her capable charge that long-ago summer. Defusing the gravest cases, from mosquito bites to homesickness, with her offbeat humor.

Just then, his dad's bronze GMC rounded the bend. At the wheel, Maggie's dad, the silver-haired former police chief, pulled alongside his son-in-law's cruiser.

Nate took a breath. "I need to help Granddad, boys."

Connor stuck his hands into his pockets. Just like Nate did. "We're okay, Daddy. You take care of Granddad."

Gemma touched Kody's shoulder. "Guys, Rascal needs to work now. I'm going to put on his PawPals vest so he knows to switch gears."

Tom Arledge unfolded from the car and shut the door gently behind him. "You need to be prepared, Nate. I've tried to calm Ike down, but…" His dark brown eyes, so like Maggie's, were sad. "Why didn't you tell us his condition had gotten so bad?"

Nate's gut knotted. "The good days were outweighing the bad. At breakfast, he was in good spirits. We were coping. I hoped with the arrival of his assistance dog…" He squeezed his eyelids closed and opened them. "Dad's a proud man. He didn't want people to know the extent of his problems."

Gemma and Rascal moved next to him. "It's natural for families to cover over the increasing deficits in order to save a loved one from awkward or embarrassing questions."

Nate looked at her. "Until they can't anymore?" But he appreciated her attempt to console him. Despite what had happened between them later, she was as kindhearted as he remembered.

Rascal rubbed his coat against Nate's leg. He found an extraordinary amount of comfort in the canine's touch.

"Nathan, I think it would be a good idea to get your dad into more familiar surroundings." She glanced at his cousins. "However, too many people right now might overstimulate him."

Bridger took off his hat. "Maggie and I can take Connor and Kody home with us for a sleepover."

Nate threw a look over his shoulder at his small sons, huddled next to Maggie. His heart twisted in his chest.

Gemma took a half step toward the boys and then as if checking herself, she stopped. "Connor and Kody have had a frightening experience. I'll do everything I can to ensure they're able to stay in their own home tonight." Compassion shone from her dark eyes. "If we're able to get the situation under control with your dad."

He nodded, grateful for her empathy for his sons. Bracing for what he might find, he opened the SUV passenger door.

Nate was taken aback by the disheveled old man glaring at him. "D-Dad?"

Looking far older than the spry, alert man he'd last seen that morning, his father was agitated and his pale blue eyes darted wildly.

"I want to go home," his father shouted.

"Dad, it's me." Anguish clawed at his throat. "It's Nate."

Lurching forward, his father would have fallen out of the vehicle if Nate hadn't grabbed his arm. "Dad, you *are* home."

"This isn't my home." His dad glowered at him. "Who are you? I want to go home. Why will no one take me home?"

He blinked rapidly. Did his father not recognize him? He'd known this moment would eventually come, but he'd never believed it would happen this soon.

Other than the ever-increasing forgetfulness, he'd believed—hoped and prayed—he and his dad would have months, if not years, together. But the disease had taken a precipitous and frightening turn for the worse.

Sudden grief rocked him. His eyes watered. He started to shake.

"Nathan." Gemma's gentle voice cut through his cloud of misery. "Don't argue with him. Go along with his reasoning. Let him know you're going to help him get home."

The steadfastness in her gaze gave him the courage to do what needed to be done.

He swallowed the sorrow he was only just keeping at bay. "I'll take you home, sir. Come with me. Okay?"

The confused old man bore no resemblance to the strong, confident rancher he had known and admired his entire life.

Eyes narrowed with suspicion, his father scrutinized his face. "You'll take me home? You promise?"

"I… I promise." In an act of sheer will, Nate quelled the quavering of his chin. "It's this way, sir." He held out his arm. "I'll show you the way home."

"Gotta get home." His dad placed his gnarled hand on Nate's coat. "Pamela's waiting supper on me."

Nate tried not to flinch. His mother died two decades ago when he was in middle school.

"If there's anything we can do…?" Tom opened his hands. "We're here for you, Nate. You're not in this alone."

On Tom's features, he caught a glimpse of the same, nearly unbearable pain welling inside himself. With slow, halting steps, he led his father toward the house.

"Connor and Kody, you come, too." Leash in hand, Gemma beckoned. "Maybe you could have a snack in the kitchen while we get your granddad settled?"

Maggie gave each boy a quick hug and nudged them toward Gemma. "Go with Rascal." She mouthed a thank-you to Gemma.

"I'll give you a call later," Nate said over his shoulder.

He helped his suddenly fragile father climb the steps to the porch. With Maggie and Tom in the cruiser, Bridger drove away.

Behind one of the posts, Gemma retrieved a small purple shoulder pack with the PawPals logo. She must have left it on the porch earlier when she'd gone in search of him.

Inside the house, he assisted his father to his favorite recliner. "Here you are, Dad."

His father's hands shook as he lowered himself into the leather chair.

Gemma ushered the boys into the kitchen. There was a soft murmur of voices, the muffled thud of a cabinet door closing, the crinkle of what had to be a potato chip bag and the clink of a glass upon the countertop.

"Where's Pam?" His dad scowled at him. "Who are you? Why are you people in my house?"

Feeling helpless, he gaped at his father.

Rascal at her side, Gemma appeared in the doorway separating the den from the kitchen. "You don't know me, Mr. Crenshaw. My name is Gemma."

She kept her voice low and soothing. "This is Rascal." She ran her hand along the collie's fur. "He's been looking forward to meeting you."

Tail wagging, Rascal barked a greeting.

A hint of something lucid—something that still belonged to the essence of the man Nate had loved his entire life—sparked in his eyes. Nate's heart jackhammered.

"Rascal?" His dad huffed, but the beginnings of a smile tilted his lips. "Earned that name, did he?"

"Well and truly." She and the dog took a single step into the room. "I'm thinking you might have more than a little in common with him. Am I right?"

Some of the strain eased from his rigid features. "Got that right. Gemma, was it?" He cocked his head.

Gemma smiled. "Yes, sir. That's right. I'm sure you have a few rascally stories you could tell."

Sticking his tongue in his cheek, his dad propped his elbows on the armrests. "I don't like to brag, mind you, but when I courted Pammie—the purtiest girl in Truelove—I gave her quite the run for her money."

Nate's mouth dropped.

Gemma threw him an amused look. "Of that, Mr. Crenshaw, there can be no doubt."

His father grinned like the mischievous charmer he'd been once upon a lifetime ago.

"I also hear you're good with dogs, Mr. Crenshaw."

His dad jutted his jaw. "I've raised a few ranch dogs in my time."

She sent Rascal toward the recliner. "Would you do me a favor and groom Rascal while I see if Miss Pamela has dinner going in the kitchen?"

Nate held his breath.

Reaching into the purple shoulder bag, she withdrew a small brush. "Rascal loved exploring your ranch this afternoon, but his coat is in need of serious attention."

Making herself small and nonthreatening, she crouched beside the collie and the chair.

She held out the brush to his dad. "Would you be a dear and help me out?"

This was the make-or-break moment. Would his dad accept Rascal into his rapidly diminishing world? Or withhold his trust?

Fear flitted across his father's face. "They're watching us, you know. They've got eyes and ears everywhere, Gemma," he hissed.

Wanting to weep at the paranoia in his dad's voice, Nate sagged heavily against the wall.

"Is it safe for Rascal here?" Brow constricting, his father's gaze pinged from Gemma to Rascal. "Safe for *me* to be here?" he whispered.

She laid the brush on the armrest next to his hand. "Rascal is here to keep you safe, Mr. Crenshaw," she whispered back.

"You promise?"

"I promise, Mr. Crenshaw."

His dad peered into her face. Slowly, the terror eased from his eyes.

"Call me Ike, short for Isaac." His father picked up the brush. "Come here, boy. Let's see what we can do to get you back to the handsome fellow I suspect you are." His dad went to work smoothing the tangles from Rascal's coat.

Getting to her feet, Gemma moved to Nate.

He crammed his hands into his coat pockets. "What do we do now?"

"We let Rascal do his job to calm your father." She turned her head toward the kitchen. "Corn chips was the quickest, if not most nutritious, snack I could find for your little guys. Why don't you get supper going while I keep an eye on your dad?"

He hunched his shoulders. "Are you sure?"

"Food would do all of us a world of good." She gave his arm a small push. "And your boys need you right now more than your father."

With his dad momentarily appeased, he joined his sons in the kitchen. He put together the most comforting, quick meal he could remember—a variation of his mother's tomato soup and grilled cheese sandwiches with thick slices of Virginia ham.

While he stirred the pot on the stove, it did not escape his notice Kody plastered himself to his side. Connor, too, attached himself like an unshakeable shadow to his every move. It had been a scary afternoon for them.

He hadn't seen them so clingy since those early weeks after Deanna died. Taking a cue from Gemma, he put the boys to work setting the kitchen table. He said a quick grace over their meal, and thanked God for bringing them home safely.

Connor picked up his sandwich. "Aren't you going to eat, Daddy?"

"You two go ahead." At the stove, he ladled soup into bowls. "I'll eat with Miss Gemma and Granddad." He placed a bowl in front of each boy.

Gemma returned to the kitchen. "That smells delicious. I think your father is ready to eat, though maybe just the soup."

He spooned a small amount into another bowl and placed it on a serving tray. He carried the tray for her. "Is Dad bonding with Rascal?" He lowered his voice. "Or is it too late? Have we already lost Dad?"

"Take a look for yourself." She took the tray from him. "Your father is a long way from lost."

His pulse pounding, he ventured into the living room. Rascal's head lay in his dad's lap. His father crooned to the collie in the baby talk people employed with animals and children. His liver-spotted hand rhythmically combed through the fur of Rascal's coat.

Both dog and man looked utterly content. His dad appeared as peaceful as he'd seen him in months.

Smiling, his father looked up. "Have you met my new friend, Rascal?" The confusion had cleared from his gaze. "Rascal's coming to live with us. Isn't that great news?"

Tears misted Nate's eyes. "The best news, Dad."

His father sniffed the air appreciably. "Is that your mother's tomato soup I smell?" He grinned at Nate. "It's not as spectacular as hers, but your version is good, too. I can't believe how hungry I am. Must have been a busy day on the ranch. What did we do today, son?"

How many more chances would he get to hear his father call him "son"?

Emotion welling in his heart, he shot a look at Gemma. "We mended fences, Dad." In more ways than one.

His father wasn't lost to them. *Thank You, God.* His dad was back. At least for now. And for now, it was enough. More than enough.

Nate's relief was so great, it nearly brought him to his knees. "Thank you, Gemma," he rasped.

She set the serving tray on a folding table next to the recliner. "Thank Rascal. He's the real hero." She stroked the collie's head.

Rascal removed himself from the older man's lap, but didn't drift far. He settled into a furry heap on top of his father's feet.

His dad chuckled. "Such a rascally pup."

She moved the tray table within easy reach of his father. "Let's leave your dad to his supper. After dinner, I promised he could feed Rascal, and we'd unpack his toys."

A lump settled in Nate's throat. "Does this mean you're staying?"

"Of course. Like Juliet told you over the phone. PawPals provides a training camp for clients."

"I don't know how we would've gotten through this afternoon without you."

"By the end of two weeks, it'll seem like Rascal has always been a part of your family. He'll aid your father in keeping his independence for as long as possible."

"Two weeks?" Suddenly, that seemed far too short a time. "After that, what will you do?"

She gave him the most curious of looks. "I'll train another neuro-service dog for the next family."

Of course. What else would she do? Their lives would go in separate directions.

He tried not to dwell on how lost he'd feel after she left Truelove.

Chapter Three

That night, Gemma was awakened by the sound of a faint, tiny beeping. Concerned, she grabbed her robe and headed out of the guest bedroom next to Ike's. At the end of the hallway lit only by the single bulb of a solitary night-light, in a T-shirt and pajama bottoms, Nathan gazed into the darkened kitchen. Moonlight cast a silvery glow through the window over the sink.

She laid her hand on his shoulder blade so as not to startle him. "Is everything all right? What's going on?"

Bare arms crossed, he leaned against the door frame. "Dad wanders at night. I installed an alarm to go off if his bedroom door opened," he whispered. "I'm sorry it woke you up."

"That's why I'm here," she whispered back. "To help you work through real-life scenarios with Rascal."

Gemma peered over his shoulder. The collie had inserted his body between Ike and the outside door. Making soft, wuffling noises, Rascal nudged Ike's pajama leg with his head.

She smiled. "Looks like Rascal has got the situation under control."

Nathan sighed. "Should I guide Dad back to bed?"

She shook her head. "Let's not intervene. This is one of Rascal's primary jobs—to ensure Ike doesn't wander outside unaccompanied. Let Rascal redirect him." She put her finger to her lips.

Whining, Rascal butted his head gently against the older gentleman until Ike appeared to rouse as if from a stupor.

Bending, Ike rubbed Rascal's head. "Are you thirsty?"

Finding Rascal's bowl, the older man carried it to the sink and filled it with water. Setting it in place beside the kitchen island, he returned to the sink and removed a glass from the cabinet. "I'm a mite thirsty, too, Rascal, my boy."

Ike took a long swig of water and placed it in the sink. He wiped his hand across his mouth. "I'm ready for bed. How about you?"

Rascal gave him a quiet woof.

With the dog by his side, Ike headed toward the hall. Gemma pulled Nathan through the open door of the bathroom. As the older man passed them, Rascal turned his head toward her. She gave the dog a small thumbs-up—the nonverbal equivalent of "good boy."

Seconds later, there was the soft snick of Ike's bedroom door closing.

"Your father will probably sleep through the rest of the night, but if not, Rascal will be there to make sure he's okay. When is the last time you had a full night's sleep?"

Nathan threw her a sheepish look. "I look that bad, huh?" He dragged his hand through his already mussed hair.

Her heart did an uptick. Nathan Crenshaw looked the opposite of bad. His bare feet poking out from his pajamas, he looked impossibly handsome.

Before the idea could take root, she squashed it.

Pulling the cords of her robe tighter, she gathered her professionalism around her like a shield. "With sundowner syndrome, it's as if the patient is in a fevered delirium from which they must be awakened. You'll find Rascal a vigilant protector of your father, keeping him safe from himself."

They moved into the hallway.

Nathan scrubbed his hand over his five-o'clock shadow. "I

don't function too well when I'm sleep-deprived. Today was a perfect example of how there's never enough of me to go around—the downed fence, forgetting the appointment with you, then what happened with Dad and the boys."

The night-light shone upon his features. Exhaustion etched itself across the lines of his face.

"What happened at school wasn't your fault. You don't give yourself enough credit." Without conscious thought, she took a step closer. "You've done everything right by your dad to ensure he's happy and safe. Installing the electronic devices… Getting him a service dog."

He looked at the closed door of his father's bedroom. "I haven't coped as well as I should. It's been overwhelming at times. The never-ending responsibility for his welfare and for the boys." His voice thickened. "I've felt so alone."

"Not anymore." She shook her head. "You have Rascal on your team now."

"And you," he rasped.

Her gaze locked onto his.

Pinpricks of awareness danced down her spine. "For two weeks…"

His gaze never left hers. "Then you'll return to Greensboro and Mr. Spencer?"

There was something unfathomable in his eyes. She felt on the cusp of throwing herself headlong into the liquid blue fire of their depths.

She pursed her lips. "There is no Mr. Spencer."

His eyebrow cocked. "Divorced, or widowed like me?"

"Neither."

He waited, as if willing her to explain. Not something she had any intention of doing. Not if she wanted to preserve his image of the Gemma she used to be. The Gemma he used to love.

After a long moment of silence, thick with unasked questions, he nodded. "I see."

But he didn't. He couldn't. Even after all these years, she only half understood it herself. There was a handful of people, including her longtime friend Juliet, who knew what happened the day she returned from summer camp that long-ago August.

A story she never intended Nathan to know. It was the reason she'd ended their relationship. She had borne so much, but the one thing she couldn't bear would be to see her shame reflected in Nathan Crenshaw's dark blue eyes. Anything but that.

"Just to be clear…" Something in his face shifted. "You're not married."

It seemed of such monumental importance to him. As if the fate of the world rested on her answer. Something raw, powerful and vulnerable rose palpably between them.

Her heart drummed in her chest.

"No," she said at last, conceding the point. "I am not, nor have I ever been married."

Clutching at the tatters of her self-respect, she spun on her heel and fled to the relative safety of the guest room. Gasping for breath as if she'd run a marathon instead of a short sprint down the hallway, she leaned against the closed door, her palms pressed flat against the panels.

She heard the muted slap of his feet as he retreated to the back of the house and the master bedroom.

Gemma struggled to capture her careening thoughts. But as her breathing gradually slowed, she wondered if what just happened was a hurdle that needed to be crossed between them. So she could finish the job she'd come to do.

She'd known when Juliet first showed her Nathan's application for a dementia assistance dog, the unresolved situation between them was likely to be fraught with dangerous undercurrents.

Yet she was good at what she did. The dogs she'd trained

over the years provided such life-changing services. She'd been unable to walk away from helping his family.

Lying on the bed unable to sleep, she went over the events of the tumultuous day.

She was pleased Rascal's training had paid off. Pleased for Rascal and Ike. Pleased for Nathan, too. It was obvious the burdens he carried were crushing him.

After eighteen months of scent-training Rascal to bond with Ike, she'd believed she was ready to walk back into Nathan's life, albeit temporarily.

Now after her visceral reaction to him and the fool she'd made of herself in running away from him, she pondered if fifteen years had been enough to get over her first and only love, Nathan Crenshaw.

Would thirty—or a lifetime—have been enough?

She stared at the ceiling above the bed. "Two weeks, Lord." It wasn't so much a statement as a plea for help.

The next morning, she let Rascal out of Ike's bedroom. The collie padded down the hall with her. In the kitchen, she found Nathan dressed for his day on the farm in jeans, his stocking feet and a long flannel shirt worn over a gray Henley.

She spied a pair of work boots by the door. He'd already been hard at work with morning chores and returned to the house. She supposed a rancher had to be an early riser. So did a dog trainer.

According to the schedule Nathan shared with her yesterday, Ike wouldn't be awake for another hour or two. Ike's midnight wanderings must have been playing havoc with Nathan's stamina.

Despite the late night, he looked far too handsome for her good. He poured water into a coffeemaker. "Gemma." His voice had an early-morning gravelly quality to it.

A sudden awkwardness sprang between them. "Nathan."

Opening the kitchen door, she let Rascal out to do his morning business. It was one of the items on her training list for Nathan to take over after she left. She reminded herself rather forcibly that she would be leaving.

Standing on the wraparound porch with its amazing three-sixty views of the mountains, the large red barn and various outbuildings, she wrapped her arms around the heather-purple sweater she'd donned. Rascal headed toward a bush.

High Country Ranch felt like such a happy, wondrous place, where nothing bad could ever affect the people who called it home. That couldn't be true, or else Rascal's services would never have been needed. Yet the feeling persisted.

With Rascal by her side, she ventured inside the farmhouse again. Minutes later, any lingering tension was broken when Connor and Kody, like two cowboy tornadoes, rushed into the kitchen.

Heading straight for her, Kody wound his arms around her waist. "Mornin', Miss Gemma."

Surprised and touched, she hugged him back. He smelled like soap and toothpaste. Just like a little boy should. Not that she'd ever had much to do with children. Unlike Juliet. Over the last few years, her dearest friend had managed to acquire a stepdaughter and a baby son of her own.

Hands crammed in his jean pockets—so like his lanky father—Connor cleared his throat. "We love having you and Rascal here, Miss Gemma."

Nathan's oldest son wasn't as exuberant a personality as his brother, but she felt the sincerity of his affection. Yet the look of anxiety on his face concerned her. A niggling spur of worry for Nathan's eldest lodged itself in her heart.

As usual, Rascal sensed the one who needed him the most. It was to Connor he went first, not Kody. The collie pushed his head under the little boy's hand. A shy smile broke across Connor's face.

For a second, the anxiety receded in his eyes. She wanted Connor to laugh and play like other little boys. She decided to make it one of Rascal's jobs to banish the concern from the child's face.

Of course, she wouldn't see it happen because she was only here two weeks. Her insides did a nosedive. Usually, she was more than ready to move on to the next dog and the next family.

"Coffee?"

Her eyes flicked to Nathan. He held a mug out to her. Something as delicate as a butterfly's wings flitted inside her chest.

The blood pounded in her ears. "Thanks," she managed to gasp. Taking the cup, she took an appreciative sip of the aromatic brew in an effort to regulate her heartbeat.

He returned to the stove. "How do you like your eggs?" His brow creased. "You like eggs for breakfast, don't you?"

Despite the charged, intense summer they'd once spent together, she realized they actually knew little of the practical things about each other. Nor anything at all about the adults they'd become.

"Gemma?" Spatula in hand, he angled toward her. "Eggs?"

"Eggs are great." She hid her face in the mug. "Any way is fine."

Kody set the table. Connor inserted bread into a toaster.

She put down the mug on the counter. "What can I do to help?" It wasn't in her nature to be idle.

Watching the eggs sizzle in the skillet, Nathan had his back to her. "I wouldn't be too quick to offer. I might put you to work shoveling cow stalls."

She heard the grin in his voice.

"As a dog trainer, I'm not afraid of hard work or a little poo."

Kody held his nose. "Too much poop, Miss Gemma."

"Thanks for the warning." She laughed. "I like all animals, although I don't know much about cattle."

"If you like, I could give you a proper tour of the ranch later."

Her eyes flitted to Nathan's and held. "I… I'd like that."

The bread popped up out of the toaster. They jerked. He turned to stir the eggs. Covering her confusion, she picked up her cup again, warming her hands around the mug.

Kody slathered butter on the slices and then cut the bread into triangles with a butter knife. Connor poured milk into glasses. The Crenshaw men were a well-oiled, breakfast-making machine.

Connor held out a chair for her. "Miss Gemma."

So well-mannered. Like every other properly reared Southern child, the "Miss" was an honorary title of respect bestowed on any elder lady. No matter if the "Miss" was elderly or not.

Due to their mother's early influence? With their short, dark hair and blue eyes, both boys were incredibly like Nate. Not that she'd ever ask, but she couldn't help wondering what had happened to their mother.

"Miss Gemma?" the little boy prompted.

Woolgathering again. The High Country Ranch and the Crenshaw men in the plural were having a completely deleterious effect on her concentration.

Since she wasn't going to be allowed to help, she sat down. "You have quite the team, Nathan."

He placed a heaping platter of scrambled eggs in the middle of the table. "They're good boys."

They were incredibly sweet boys.

Everyone sat down. The boys bowed their heads. Nathan said grace.

Between bites of eggs and toast, she tried to get to know the boys better. She asked the usual questions about their teachers, who were their best friends and what they liked the most about school.

As she watched the loving interaction between Nathan and

his sons, a strange longing tugged at her heartstrings. Sitting at the table, sharing their lives with each other, it was the kind of family she always wished had been hers.

If her world hadn't fractured that long-ago August and she hadn't ended things with Nathan, a family like this might have become hers.

Connor and Kody would never fully comprehend how blessed they were to have a man like Nathan as their dad. A man the exact opposite of her own father. Remembered shame burned her cheeks. She kept her head over her plate.

No child of hers would ever endure a childhood like she'd endured. Because she would never put herself in the same situation as her mother. Her eyes strayed to Nathan. No matter how handsome or winsome the cowboy rancher.

Best to keep a professional aloofness. After two weeks, she'd never see any of the Crenshaws again. Which, given her conflicted feelings for Nathan, was just as well. Yet somehow the idea of not seeing any of them again failed to cheer her as she'd hoped it might.

At the end of the meal, she insisted on cleaning up the dishes. With his nose, Rascal pushed a small red ball across the linoleum to Connor's chair.

The boy looked at her.

Scraping plates, she smiled at him. "Until your granddad gets up, Rascal would love to play with you."

"Yay!" Kody fist-pumped the air.

Connor's blue eyes flickered. "We need to make our lunches, Kode. So Daddy doesn't have to, remember?"

The kindergartener's face fell. "I forgot."

She handed Nathan the plates. "Let me make the lunches."

Frowning, Nathan stacked the plates in the dishwasher. "Gemma…"

"No, really." She held up her hand. "I want to."

And she did. Truly. More than was sensible. But suddenly, she didn't care. Not if it brought happiness to Nathan's little guys.

She tilted her head and looked at him. "Please?"

He gave her a bemused smile. "I never could refuse you anything when you turned those big, puppy-dog brown eyes on me."

Gemma's heart skipped a beat.

He ruffled Connor's hair. "Go ahead, son. Have fun with Rascal."

Kody did a silly sort of happy dance.

"Thank you, Daddy." Connor included her in the ecstatic smile he threw his father. "Miss Gemma."

His tail wagging like a flag in a stiff breeze on the Fourth of July, Rascal appeared to know playtime was on the horizon. To Connor's and Kody's delight, he covered their faces with doggy slobber. They chortled.

She opened the fridge and examined the contents. "Turkey, cheese, lettuce and mayo work for you guys today?"

Kody grabbed the red ball. "Yes, ma'am. Please."

Her heart warmed. They'd done their Southern mama proud. Good boys. Such good, sweet, dear boys.

Nathan pulled two insulated lunch boxes off a shelf in the pantry.

"Guys, roll the ball along the floor and Rascal will retrieve it." She spread mayonnaise on slices of bread. "He loves nothing better than playing fetch." She glanced at their father.

Leaning against the countertop sipping his coffee, Nathan was quiet, quieter than the pay-for-every-word boy she recalled. A slight smile curved his lips as he watched the boys play with the collie.

She felt his eyes drift in her direction. A curiosity about her gleamed in his dark blue gaze. A curiosity she didn't intend to satisfy.

Outside, a green Subaru drove up. A horn tooted. The boys grabbed their backpacks off the back of their chairs. There was a sudden stampede for jackets. An onslaught of frantic hugs for Rascal and their dad.

Stepping onto the porch, she handed them their lunch boxes, which resulted in equally fervent, if unexpected, hugs for her, too.

Calling goodbye, the boys dashed toward the vehicle. A window scrolled down. Maggie stuck out her hand and waved. Gemma made out the silhouettes of two other little boys in the back seat. As befitted his position as eldest cousin, Connor got to ride shotgun in the front.

Then, doors closed, seat belts secured, Maggie steered the car back the way she'd come.

As the red taillights of the Subaru disappeared in the early-morning mist, Gemma stared after them, a trifle gobsmacked.

She sensed rather than saw Nathan at her elbow. She possessed a weird sort of radar whenever he moved into close proximity.

Gemma shook her head. "How does Ike manage to sleep through this ruckus every morning?"

Nathan chuckled. "Connor and Kody are a lot." But the fatherly pride in his voice was unmistakable.

"They're wonderful," she whispered.

"Yeah, they are." He smiled. "We've got time before Dad stirs. How about that ranch tour?"

She really ought to get to work—the sooner she did her job, the sooner she could return to PawPals. But when he looked at her like that…

For once, she decided aloofness might be overrated.

Chapter Four

On the porch, Nate wished almost immediately he hadn't offered to show her around the farm.

Earlier, she'd indicated interest. He flushed. Interest in the High Country Ranch. Not in him, of course. Which was exactly as it should be.

His resentment at how she'd dumped him fifteen years ago—even now with no explanation—rankled.

She'd been so good with the boys this morning, for a second he forgot how clear she'd been about maintaining professional boundaries. A reminder he'd do well to heed. How had he already managed to overstep?

He had neither the time, energy or inclination for anything beyond his responsibilities to his sons, his father and the ranch.

Just as he was working his way to a clumsy retraction—

"Let me grab a jacket…" She gave him a faint smile. "I'll leave Rascal to watch over Ike in case he awakens while we're gone." The hinges squeaking, she eased through the door.

Hunching his shoulders, he stuffed his hands into his jean pockets. Hinges creaking, she closed the door softly behind her and joined him on the porch.

She held out his coat. "You might need this."

Blinking, he took his coat from her. "Thanks."

She rubbed her hands together. "It's colder here than Greensboro."

"We're at a higher elevation." He slipped into his coat. "The mountain peaks will get the first dusting of snow soon, but it will be several weeks for those of us in the valley."

She studied the mountain range in the distance. "I won't be here to see it."

He felt the gentle, altogether necessary, admonishment like a kick in the gut.

Stick to business, Crenshaw. She wants to see the ranch, not reconnect on a personal level. Jerking his mind from golden blond hair and silk ribbons, he set his jaw and moved down the steps.

"How many cattle do you have?"

Nate led her toward the livestock buildings. "We have over a hundred and fifty cows on our four hundred acres."

"Wow." She took in the acreage as he pointed out the hay storage sheds, water tanks, feeding facilities and calving barn.

Beyond the small pond, he drew her closer to one of the grazing pastures. At the fence line, he opened the gate, stepped into the paddock and beckoned her.

She gave the herd of cattle a hesitant look.

"It's okay. The cows are used to people. Hand raised, they are my first and last stop every day."

She ventured into the pasture, and he shut the gate behind her. Taking a few steps, he held out his hand and gave a low whistle. One of the cows disengaged from the herd and ambled over to them.

He grinned at the expression on her face. "The cattle are trained to follow us so we're able to move them from pasture to pasture every day or two without stressing them with chasing or herding." He rested the flat of his hand on the cow's broad black shoulder. "Go ahead and touch her if you want."

Biting her bottom lip, Gemma laid her hand on the cow. A smile teased at the edges of her lips. The breeze ruffled wisps of her hair.

For a second, time went sideways. He'd come home at the end of that summer imagining her eventually joining him on the farm. Surrounded by these mountains. Raising cattle and a family. By his side. And now, here she was.

His heart clenched painfully in his chest. It hadn't been Gemma who joined him on the ranch. It had been Deanna with whom he'd made a life. A pang of unanticipated grief assailed him. Followed by a wave of guilt.

"What kind of cattle do you raise?"

Startled out of his painful reverie, he dragged his attention to the present.

"It's a mixed-breed operation. Red and Black Angus. Hereford. And Charolais."

Shading her hand over her eyes, she peered out over the hilly terrain and the distant fallow fields. "I didn't realize cattle ranching involved farming the land, too."

"We take pasture-to-plate seriously. Our cattle are pasture fed year-round. Raised on high-energy, high-protein sweet-grasses. No feedlots. Hormone free. Antibiotic free."

He moved among the herd, doing his daily check to make sure each one was in optimal condition. She strolled after him.

"We grow our own forage. Last month, we harvested the last crop. This time of year, they feed on rye grass, crimson and red clover."

"This is quite the operation." She smiled at him. His chest squeezed. "I'm impressed."

"High Country Ranch is a fifth-generation farm. It's about sustainability and good stewardship." He gazed toward the mountain vista. "I'm always mindful of our impact on the land. I want to be able to pass on to Connor, Kody and future generations the option to farm like my father passed on to me."

"You enjoy working the land, don't you?"

He looked at her. "I do." He laughed. "When I was in high

school, I couldn't wait to get out of Truelove and experience real—" he made quote marks in the air with his fingers "—life."

"You've made a good life for yourself here." She made a sweeping motion. "This is the realest, the best, life can offer."

A good life. Exactly what he and Deanna had carved out here when they took over primary responsibility for the farm. Although without Deanna, it also had become a lonely one.

Nate cut his eyes at Gemma. She had her dogs and her work. Was it enough for her? Did she ever feel lonely, too?

He'd never needed to wonder about his wife's feelings on any subject matter. They'd been high school sweethearts. A former cheerleader, Deanna had been openhearted, bubbly and animated. He'd never had to doubt where he stood with her.

Yet the spring of his junior year, he'd been restless and dissatisfied with what he perceived as the boring sameness of small-town life. Heading off to work as a camp counselor that summer, he'd broken up with Deanna. Ironic. He'd done to her what Gemma would later do to him.

Gemma was quieter than Deanna had been. The lovely dog trainer wasn't one to broadcast her emotions.

As the sun climbed higher on the horizon, she put her hand over her brow to shade her eyes. "What changed your mind about farming?"

She had.

But they no longer knew each other well enough for that conversation. In light of her subsequent rejection, he doubted he'd ever known Gemma as well as he believed.

That summer changed his life forever. He'd loved her so blindly and devotedly. He was old enough now to recognize there had been moments when he'd sensed she kept parts of herself hidden.

He flicked a glance in her direction. Perhaps the mystery had been a large part of his attraction. Until her secrets drove them apart for good.

After the breakup, he'd thrown himself into the backbreaking work of the ranch. Initially he was hurt beyond belief, but anger at Gemma's treatment of him soon followed. True to her forgiving nature, Deanna had been quick to console him. Her utter devotion had gone a long way toward soothing his pride and filling the hole in his heart. A few months later, he and Deanna got together again.

Gemma blew out a breath. "You don't work the ranch by yourself, do you?"

He squinched his eyes against the glow of the sun. "Dad used to help."

She tilted her head. "It seems a lot for just you and your dad."

It hadn't always been only him and his dad. There'd been Deanna, too.

"Every year, the boys are able to help more." He scrubbed his hand over his face. "I can handle everything else."

Forehead puckering, she gave the red-and-white Hereford steer a final pat. "We should probably check on Rascal and your dad."

Opening the gate, he allowed her to precede him before latching it behind them.

Rounding the corner of the house, she paused beside the small, fenced-off garden area. "What vegetables do you grow?"

"Not vegetables." His jaw tightened. "Deanna liked flowers."

After her death, one by one the flowers she'd loved had faded and wilted from neglect.

Sometimes in the wee hours of the night when he couldn't sleep, he regretted how often he'd taken her for granted. Unable to bear the reminders of her absence, he'd plowed the little garden under. Although for some reason, he hadn't yet dismantled the deer fence around it.

"Your wife's name was Deanna?" Gemma gave him a gentle smile. "A lovely name."

"She was a lovely person," he rasped.

He couldn't bring himself to talk to Gemma about his late wife. It felt too much like a betrayal.

Her face fell as she got a nice view of his back. Message received loud and clear. He didn't want to talk about his wife. He must have loved Deanna so much if he couldn't bring himself to speak of her.

What must it be like to have been loved like that? Not something she'd ever experienced. Her stomach clenched. Not something she would ever experience if the current state of her life—PawPals and her beloved dogs—was any indication of what her future held.

Head down, she trailed after him. Inside the kitchen, he toed out of his heavy-duty work boots. Following his example, she slipped out of her low-ankle muck boots.

Nathan busied himself at the sink. "Dad must still be asleep."

She shrugged out of her coat. "The late night is catching up with Ike."

His broad, muscled shoulders slumped. "With us all." He hadn't bothered to remove his jacket.

She gripped the back of one of the chairs. "If you've work to do, I'll stay here until your father gets up."

He did an about-face, pressing against the countertop. "I've always got work to do, but I should be here in case he wakes up disoriented."

Maybe the ranch wasn't financially secure. Perhaps there was no money to hire someone to help him. It was none of her business.

His lips thinned. "Is there stuff we should be going over while we're stuck—I mean, waiting?"

Stuck with her. Gone was the comfortable camaraderie they'd shared in the pasture. All traces of the easygoing, sweet boy she'd known were gone. Vanished once the conversation had drifted to...his wife?

Or was the stiffness between them about something else?

Her heart slammed against her rib cage. "About what happened last night..."

Nathan stiffened. "Rascal made a real difference for my dad. Won't be long before you can return to your own life."

Leaving him to his? She flushed. *Right back at you, Nathan Crenshaw.*

Irritation burned at her stomach. To him, she was nothing more than an unwelcome intrusion. Another item to be checked off on his to-do list.

Two weeks... She'd likely never see the Crenshaws, father, son and grandsons, ever again. He didn't want her gone any more than she wanted to be gone. But until that time—

"Maybe now would be a good time to go over prepping your dad's medication each morning." She squared her shoulders. "That will need to be done before you head out at the crack of dawn to begin your never-ending chores."

He gave her a look that could have scorched milk. "Fine." He yanked out the chair across the table and threw himself into it.

Glaring back at him, she pulled out a chair and plopped down.

Clearly, he wasn't the same boy she remembered. Which was all well and good because she wasn't the same naive, mooned-eyed innocent she used to be, either.

She had a job to do. Her only concern must remain fixed on Ike and on Rascal's ability to help him.

"I think it would be wise to update Ike's doctor on yesterday's events." She laid her palms flat upon the surface of the table. Proud that her hands didn't shake. Nor her voice wobble. "His prescription may need adjusting."

Nathan gave her a curt nod. "I'll make the appointment. It'd be great if you could go with us to the appointment to clarify the role Rascal will have in my father's treatment plan. Not sure if the doc will have an opening this week, though." His eyes darkened to indigo, the color of the sky before a coming storm. "But I know how difficult you find commitment."

Was his chip-on-the-shoulder attitude about their history with each other? About that summer—their summer? He'd moved on. She had, too.

Hadn't they?

Juliet had warned her. This had been a mistake. A bad idea for Gemma to take on this case. Yet she was here now. There was no one else. What was done was done.

She darted a glance at the set, closed expression on his face. Done in more ways than merely the present.

Gemma took a deep breath. "If I'm unable to be here for the appointment, maybe the doctor and I could teleconference."

A muscle throbbed in his cheek.

"The program will not succeed if we don't work as a team. If that isn't something *you* can commit to, tell me now."

Their gazes locked. And held for a long, long moment. She didn't dare breathe or break eye contact. She mustn't back down. For Ike's sake, this was too important.

Plowing his hand through his hair, Nathan was the first to look away. "I apologize. I'll do everything in my power to make this work for my dad." His gaze returned to hers. "This won't be a problem again."

This—the energy between them last night? The amiable companionship this morning?

"I apologize, too."

Gemma had learned the hard way it was better to know where she stood with people. She'd been forced to grow up rapidly in the space of one horrific day. With Nathan, now she knew. Boundary lines had been drawn. She would respect them.

Scraping her chair across the linoleum, she retrieved Ike's medicine bottles and went over what he needed to do to help Rascal do his job. She also hammered out what the rest of Ike's day should look like.

True to his word, nothing further was said of the electrifying moment between them last night. For which she was grateful.

Later that morning, he was able to secure an appointment with Ike's doctor, who specialized in neurodegenerative disorders, for the following Monday.

Over the next few days, she worked with Rascal to be of most service to Ike. By unspoken mutual agreement, she and Nathan kept their distance. A painful politeness.

When forced to interact on Ike's behalf or at dinner with the boys, they remained cordial. Otherwise, the farm was a big place. It wasn't hard to avoid each other.

Each morning, Rascal acted as Ike's canine alarm clock, urging him out of bed. At the sound of an electronic timer, Rascal brought a bag of medicine to Ike, which included a note reminding him to take the pills with a glass of water.

Thankfully, Ike was still ambulatory and took care of his own hygiene needs. Yet she trained Rascal to wait for Ike outside the shower and taught him how to trigger a specially installed alarm should the older gentleman experience a problem.

Most of all, Rascal provided a constant source of encouragement and companionship that was truly making a difference in Ike's slowly returning self-confidence. Putting a larger harness on Rascal to aid Ike's balance over the rough terrain of the ranch, she instituted midafternoon walks around the pastures. The exercise was good for Ike's mental and physical well-being. The timing of the walk served to tire him out enough so that sleep came more readily at bedtime.

Sometimes she caught sight of Nathan near the grazing herd or by one of the barns. He'd assured her winter was his slower time on the ranch, yet out of necessity he was out on the farm most of the day. If she hadn't been at the farmhouse, Ike would have been left on his own.

Rascal was trained to respond to a caregiver's commands, but between the demands of the ranch and his children, Nathan wasn't always available to direct Rascal or perform the tasks only a human could do.

Ike's illness had reached the stage where the lack of a full-time caregiver was a growing concern to her. Ike's doctor should be aware of how much time he spent on his own, but she wanted to address her misgivings with Nathan first.

He would accuse her of interfering. He'd be angry, but Ike's safety was paramount. Her apprehension wasn't only for his father. Nathan's long-term well-being was at stake, too.

Illnesses like Ike's often took the greatest toll on their caregivers. And if something happened to Nathan, what would become of his motherless sons?

Living with a loved one's dementia meant endless hard conversations between everyone concerned. But the coming confrontation threatened to sever her tenuous truce with Nathan.

Ike experienced only one other episode that first week. The structure of the daily routine she'd implemented was working.

The outdoor air and the healing benefits of nature countered some of the sundowner syndrome triggers. As soon as Rascal sensed an oncoming bout of agitation, the dog refocused Ike's attention by bringing him the brush. It helped Ike to have something to occupy his hands. Gemma hoped to have hit on a strategy to avert another crisis like the one to which she'd arrived.

Ike responded well to the new routine. She posted Ike's schedule on the refrigerator and went over the details with his family.

Each afternoon when Maggie brought Connor and Kody

home, she enjoyed hearing about their day at school. It hadn't taken long for the boys to make a special place for themselves within her heart.

Those first few days she'd stuck close to Ike in case she was needed. But later in the week, she let Rascal get on with his job, and she spent more time outside.

While Ike took his afternoon nap, she wandered around the farm. While they did their chores after school, Connor and Kody liked to show her around. She didn't mind in the slightest.

Kody had joined the local 4-H chapter only recently. In one of the outbuildings, he introduced her to his two rabbits. He was raising the fluffy white rabbits with black ears to show at the county fair next spring.

"I helped Daddy build the wabbit hutch." Kody's chest puffed with pride. "'Cause in 4-H you learn by doing."

"And you did a terrific job." Admiring his handiwork on the raised plywood hutch, she smiled at the little boy. "It's a rabbit palace for bunnies."

Kody grinned. "It's my job to feed them and make sure they have enough water." He pointed to the larger rabbit, nibbling on a piece of timothy hay. "That's Sir Hops-a-Lot."

She laughed. "What's the other one's name?"

"Harriet. *H-a...*" He looked at Connor.

Connor's lips quirked. *"H-a-r-e."*

"A hare is like saying, 'wabbit.' Did you know that, Miss Gemma?"

"I did know that, Kody."

Chortling at his own joke, he slapped his hand on his knee. "Aren't I funny, Miss Gemma?"

She tapped the end of his nose. "The funniest five-year-old I know."

"It was Granddad who thought of those names, Kode." Connor dropped his gaze. "Before he got so sick."

Kody's shoulders drooped. "I miss the stuff we used to do with him."

Connor sighed. "Grandad took us to our 4-H meeting every week."

Kody's bottom lip wobbled. "Granddad was helping me keep a wecord of Hops-a-Lot and Hare-i-et's progress for the fair 'cause I can't write yet."

Connor squeezed his brother's shoulder. "I told you I'd help you. It'll be okay, bud. No need for you to worry."

Her eyes misted. They were such good brothers to each other.

"I miss him," Connor whispered. "The way he used to be."

A single, solitary tear rolled down Kody's cheek. "When he gets confused, it's makes me afwaid."

She wrestled with what to say to them. With how to comfort them.

"Your grandad's disease *is* confusing. For grown-ups, too. And scary."

Crouching, she put an arm around both boys and hugged them. "But no matter what, I know your granddad loves you so much."

Kody burrowed into her. "Granddad is going to die, isn't he, Miss Gemma? Just like our mom."

Her heart clenched.

Connor frowned. "Don't talk about stuff like that, Kode. It's too sad."

She shook her head. "It's okay to feel sad about what your grandfather is going through, guys. If you're feeling scared or sad, it helps to talk about it."

Connor's brow furrowed. "How do you know?"

She swallowed. "Something scary happened to me when I was younger. I didn't tell anyone how confused and afraid and angry I was."

The boys looked at her.

She took a deep breath. "I believed I was being brave by never crying or talking about it, but now I think it would've been better if I had. I would've felt better sooner."

Connor nodded slowly, and she could tell he was thinking through what she had said. Very much like how his father processed everything.

Kody rested his head against her shoulder. "I like talking with you, Miss Gemma."

Her lips brushed against his forehead. "I like talking to you, too, Kody."

Connor leaned into her side. "Rascal is helping Granddad feel better."

She gave him a bright smile. "I'm praying with Rascal's help, you will make many more happy memories together."

Kody straightened. "Would you like to hold Sir Hops-a-Lot while I clean his cage? He's really soft."

She smiled at Kody. "Until I go check on Rascal and your granddad, I'd love to hold Sir Hops-a-Lot."

Gemma took a seat on a nearby bale of straw. At a sudden creak, she looked over her shoulder at the shadows near the door. There was no one there. Probably just the wind.

Opening the hutch, Kody extricated the rabbit and gently deposited his pet into her lap. He handed off Hare-i-et to Connor, who sank down beside her.

She ran her fingers through the silky coat of the bunny's fur.

Kody got busy cleaning out the hutch. "Sir Hops-a-Lot is a buck." Going into professor mode, he wagged his finger at her. "That's a boy wabbit. Hare-i-et is a doe, a girl wabbit."

"You are a bunny expert, Kody."

Connor groaned. "Don't encourage him."

She laughed. "I don't mind."

Connor brushed the tip of his finger along the rabbit's head. "My ultimate goal is to someday raise alpacas."

Alpacas? She smothered a grin.

"But until then, Daddy says the next calf born will be my 4-H project." He jutted his chin. "I can show calves next year because I'll be eight."

"Absolutely."

Connor gave her a rare smile. "I'm so happy you came to help Granddad, Miss Gemma."

Her eyes misted. "Me, too."

Despite the awkwardness between her and their father, she wouldn't have missed getting to know his sons for the world.

As for Nathan?

She buried her face in the soft fluff of Sir Hops-a-Lot.

Gemma learned a long time ago it was less painful to not dwell on what couldn't be changed. Like once-upon-a-time-dreams that could never come true.

Chapter Five

Nate hadn't meant to eavesdrop.

He'd gone in search of the boys and heard their voices in the barn with the rabbit hutch. He'd been about to step out of the shadows when he caught wind of their conversation with Gemma.

It killed him to hear the sadness and confusion in their little voices. He'd tried so hard to make sure they didn't suffer the lack of anything during his dad's illness and after their mother's death.

One more thing at which he'd fallen short. When the discussion took a lighter turn, he decided to beat a hasty retreat. He didn't want her to feel uncomfortable.

When he took a backward step, the floorboard creaked. He froze. Silence fell for a second, but his sons soon picked up the conversation with Gemma again.

Breathing a sigh of relief, he slipped out the door. Trudging to the house, he checked on his dad. At his approach, Rascal lifted his head from a recumbent position outside his father's bedroom. With the situation under control thanks to Rascal, he moved to the porch to wait for his sons.

From her talk with the boys, it appeared she had suffered a traumatizing loss of her own. At the time, he'd assumed she broke things off with him because she'd met someone else.

Nate scrubbed his face with his hand. Had something else

happened after they returned from camp that summer? Even after all these years, it pained him to think of her being hurt. Though from what, he had no idea.

He'd always heard a person never quite got over a first love. He wasn't ready to go that far, but if he was being honest, he'd admit his feelings for her weren't as nonexistent as he'd like to believe.

Might there have been extenuating circumstances to explain why she'd broken off their relationship? But then there was the added mystery of why she'd changed her name…

For the first time, the long-simmering anger he'd felt at her treatment of him diminished, leaving in its place compassion for whatever it was she'd gone through. Giving him a different perspective on their mutual past.

At the sound of footfalls, he looked up.

Catching sight of him on the top step, Gemma paused. "Is everything okay with Ike?"

He rose. "Still resting. Rascal's got everything well in paw."

Either not getting his joke, or failing to appreciate the humor, she made as if to move past him. "That's good."

Something pinched in his chest. He hadn't enjoyed the strain between them this week. "Gemma…"

She stopped.

"I accidentally overheard you talking with the boys."

She crossed her arms over her black puffy vest.

He put up his hand. "I wasn't spying on you, but you addressed their concerns so well I hesitated to interrupt. I've said as much to them before, but perhaps they needed reassurance from someone besides me."

She frowned.

"Thank you for talking with them. You knew just what to say. You're great with children."

"You think so?" Dropping her defensive posture, she looked

down and then up at him. "I wasn't sure what to say. I merely spoke from my heart."

"Exactly the right thing to do with kids. They can spot phony or insincere a mile off." And because he couldn't resist probing a tad, he continued, "You must have experience with kids."

She shook her head. "I don't. Other than spending time with Juliet and her brood."

Ah. Never married. No kids.

"Good instincts then." He smiled. "You'd make them a good mother."

She threw him a startled look.

"I didn't mean Connor or Kody... Um, kids of your own. One day."

Open mouth, insert boot.

She blinked at him.

Nate flushed. "I wasn't trying to...imply...presume..."

Stop talking, just stop talking.

He was a grown man. Why did Gemma always reduce him to a stammering teenager?

"I didn't think you were—" her gaze went everywhere except to him "—implying anything."

He jammed his hands in his pockets. "Good."

"I don't have kids in my life." Her eyes found his. "I have dogs."

"Right. Of course."

Nate loved a dog as good as the next guy, but he wouldn't trade his sons for anything else in the world. He hoped her life wasn't as lonely as she'd made it sound.

He exhaled. "Okay."

She took a step, but stopped again. "Can I ask you a question?"

"Turnabout is fair play." But he braced. For what he wasn't sure—a question about Deanna or their summer?

"First, let me say I'm amazed at what you do around the

ranch." She fluttered her hand in the direction of the pasture. "The boys. Your father."

He sensed a *but* coming. "I'm a jack of all trades. Master of none."

"Would you consider hiring someone to help with your dad?"

"You mean a full-time caregiver?" He started to bow up. "Now that we have Rascal, he's doing fine."

"Just one of the three enormous responsibilities you deal with on a daily basis would overwhelm most people." She ticked off the items on her fingers. "Running a cattle business. Raising two kids. Taking care of an ailing parent. You are stretched so thin. As for the stress… I'm worried about you, Nathan."

He bristled. "That was the whole point in having Rascal—to look after Dad. Are you telling me Rascal isn't up to the task?"

She stiffened. "Dementia assistance dogs are trained to work best under the direction of a care manager."

He narrowed his eyes. "Which would be me."

"But you're not in the house with Ike or Rascal. You're not available most of the day."

He went rigid. "I'm always available whenever he needs me."

"Due to the nature of this illness, your father's judgment about his own abilities will become increasingly impaired. He's going to become dependent on having someone on hand to safeguard him from himself. I don't know your financial situation—"

"No. You don't." He gritted his teeth. "Yet after fifteen years, you think you know me well enough to tell me how bad I'm failing my family?"

"That's not what I meant. No one is blaming you for any of this."

"Your job is to train dogs." He jabbed his finger. "It's my job to take care of my family."

She tossed her braid over her shoulder. "If there's an emergency, the system with Rascal breaks down. When he can't locate you, Rascal can't do his job of safeguarding your dad."

He scowled.

"Caring for a dementia patient takes a tremendous toll on the caregiver's mental and physical health. The impact can be long-term. It's okay to ask for help."

"I've asked for help," he growled. "Maggie has been a godsend in getting the boys to and from school."

She touched his sleeve. "Would you at least consider taking on help around the ranch? It would free you to spend more time with your father and the boys."

He wanted to hold on to his anger, but standing close to her, he felt the sincerity of her concern. He wasn't good about asking for help. No more so than his dad. Pride? A misplaced self-sufficiency?

She wasn't wrong about his boys needing him more. Not wanting to burden him with their fears, they'd reached out to her, a virtual stranger, instead of their father.

He was struck by the kindness and empathy in her eyes. No judgment. Only a desire to help. "I'll… I'll give it some thought."

"I know you'll do the right thing. You always do."

Her smile lit up her face. And places in his heart he'd believed forever numb.

Nate didn't always do the right thing. The right thing would have been to follow up with Gemma. After the Dear John voicemail, he should have checked to make sure she was okay. Especially when she refused to answer his phone calls or letters. She hadn't been okay. After they left camp, something had happened to her.

But he'd been seventeen, insecure and unsure of himself.

He let her down. Was he doomed to always fail the people he loved? He'd failed Deanna. Would he fail his father and the boys?

"How about letting me make you guys my world-famous tortellini soup for supper?"

Nate shuffled his boots on the porch step. "Gemma—"

"You didn't ask." She wagged her finger at him. "I offered. Since this asking-for-help business comes hard for you. Baby steps, Crenshaw. Baby steps."

He threw her a sheepish grin. "If you insist."

Smiling, she opened the door. "I insist." She headed into the house.

His grin fell. When it came to the lovely K-9 trainer, he couldn't help wondering what else baby steps might lead to.

After the confrontation with Nathan, the tension between them lessened.

To a degree. Yet like an unscalable boulder, the past—their shared past—loomed large and immovable between them.

Since she would only be here a little over a week longer, it was probably best not to address it. As a K-9 trainer, she knew the value of letting sleeping dogs lie. Admitting what happened would serve no purpose other than to bring up painful memories she preferred not to recall.

On Monday, she, Rascal and Ike rode with Nathan to the doctor's appointment in Asheville, an hour's drive from Truelove. She laid out the PawPals program with the doctor. Ike testified to the difference Rascal was already making in his life. Nathan expressed his concerns about the latest incident.

When she explained the need for a full-time caregiver, both Ike and Nathan became indignant.

The doctor listened carefully to each of their views and changed Ike's medication in the hope of avoiding future incidents like what happened at the school.

"For now, let's agree to monitor the situation." The neurologist cleared his throat. "If further changes are necessary, please don't hesitate to contact me."

The return trip to Truelove ride was far less pleasant than the ride to Asheville. Nathan and Ike were irritated with her. Yet later that day, Nathan contacted his friend Clay McKendry, at the nearby Bar None Ranch.

They worked out an agreement to share the fellow rancher's part-time ranch hands, splitting mornings and afternoons between the ranches. It took only a day for her to see a tremendous difference in the workload Nathan previously shouldered alone. Already, he appeared less stressed and better able to cope with his father's situation and his sons' boundless energy.

Ike wasn't one to hold a grudge. They soon returned to the easy camaraderie they'd shared before the appointment. To her relief, Nathan got over his resentment at her interference, too. But no more was said of hiring a full-time caregiver.

Despite her best intentions to steer clear of him as much as possible, she got into a routine of sorts with Nathan. She looked forward to the early mornings before the boys joined them for breakfast, when it was just her and Nathan, sharing the details of their upcoming day over coffee.

By mutual unspoken agreement, their conversations revolved around the people they'd become, rather than the teenagers they'd once been. She concentrated on getting to know the adult Nathan better. There was much to admire about a man determined to take care of his ailing father, raise his sons and run a cattle ranch.

He hadn't lost his sense of humor. He was a man of faith. A man who honored his commitments.

They talked about everything, except the past and his late wife. On some level it would have pained her to hear details of his blissful life with Deanna. But his unwillingness to talk about her at all felt like a hugely significant omission.

When Maggie brought the boys to the ranch each afternoon, Gemma liked being the first person to welcome them home. She and Maggie also got into the habit of chatting a few minutes. She'd never been one to make friends easily, but she felt she'd made a friend in Nathan's second cousin. Several years ago as a sideline, Maggie's police chief husband had started a training kennel. Sometimes if a particular canine turned out to not be suited for law enforcement work, he referred a dog to Juliet and PawPals. Gemma hadn't made the connection at first, but several of Bridger's dogs had become incredible service companions.

During the first week of training, her goal had been to help Ike and Rascal acclimate to each other. Now she was ready to tackle how Rascal might benefit Ike outside his home environment. An active social life went a long way toward diminishing the sense of isolation and bouts of depression.

One morning while the boys were at school, she, Nathan and Ike sat down to discuss what could be done with Rascal's help to give Ike a fuller life. Or at least, she and Ike sat down. Nathan leaned against the doorframe leading to the kitchen. He wasn't a man who knew how to relax.

Her job was to listen to a client's felt needs and if feasible, create a plan to meet those needs. One of the things Ike mentioned was how much he missed the weekly lunch gathering at a local diner with a group called the ROMEOs.

She glanced at Nathan.

"Retired Older Men Eating Out." He grinned. *"R-O-M-E-O."*

She laughed. "That sounds like fun."

Ike chuckled. "We're a fun group."

Folding his arms across his green-checked flannel shirt, Nathan propped against the wall. "The men have been a part of Dad's life long before any of them retired."

Ike nodded. "It's really an excuse to get together. And eat at the Mason Jar, of course."

Gemma smiled. "I'm beginning to see where Kody gets his appetite."

Seated in his recliner, Ike patted Rascal's head. "Some of the guys, like Nash and Dwight, I've known since we were boys. Tom, of course, is family. We do service projects, too." Sighing, he leaned back. "Since my driving privileges were suspended—" he shot a glance at his son "—and rightly so, I guess my ROMEO days are over."

Perched on the sofa, she jotted a few notes on her electronic tablet. "Perhaps not. At this stage in your illness, with Rascal by your side and appropriate safety protocols, I see no reason for you to be continually confined to the ranch, Ike."

A slow smile spread across Ike's grizzled features. "I sure would enjoy the opportunity to jaw with my old pals again." He winked at her. "The Double Name Club may think they run this town, but it's the ROMEOs who provide the elbow grease necessary for it to flourish."

"Double Name Club?" She cut a look at Nathan. "Is that like a garden club? Or a book club?"

Ike hooted.

"Not exactly." Nathan laughed. "The Double Name Club are in a category of their own."

Ike grinned. "The Double Name Club are also known as the Truelove matchmakers."

Nathan nodded. "The seventy-something ladies are infamous for poking their powdered noses where they don't belong. They take the town motto—Truelove, Where True Love Awaits—a little too seriously."

She raised her eyebrow.

Nathan rolled his eyes. "Half the town marriages are the result of their scheming."

His father snorted. "Half and counting. Their tally sheet also includes multigenerational matrimonial mayhem." He threw out his hands. "Not that I'm complaining. Aunt Georgie is the one who introduced Pammie and me."

In his stocking feet, their son smiled. "The founding members are GeorgeAnne Allen, ErmaJean Hicks and IdaLee Moore."

Southerners, past and current generations, were fond of double names.

Gemma shrugged. "It's nice they care so much about their friends."

"They're a menace." Nathan rubbed the back of his neck. "The matchmaking double-name cronies are determined to help everyone in Truelove find their happily-ever-after. Whether the recipients of their efforts want them to or not."

His elbows on the armrest, Ike sat forward. "My aunt, GeorgeAnne—her family owns the local hardware store—is the de facto leader of the pack."

"Your aunt?" Gemma tilted her head. "If she's in her seventies and you're—"

"Not." Ike chuckled. "Not yet anyway. Back in the day, Appalachian farm families were big of necessity. Like many others, the Arledge clan had nine children, strung out over a dozen years. Tom's daddy was the eldest son. GeorgeAnne is the oldest girl. My mama was a middle daughter." He gestured toward the ridge of mountains outside the window. "The equestrian riding center over yonder belongs to the youngest sister, CoraFaye, who's closer to my age than her own siblings."

Gemma's mouth fell open. "Wow."

Nathan grinned. "Maybe I should draw you a family tree."

"That's a lot of family." She blinked at the men. "You must be related to nearly the entire town. How wonderful."

Ike smiled. "By blood or by marriage, we probably are."

"Not so wonderful." Nathan grimaced. "Growing up, it meant

was there was nowhere someone wasn't waiting to report any misdeeds to your parents."

She arched her eyebrow. "I find it hard to believe the ultratrustworthy Nathan Crenshaw ever got up to misdeeds."

"Just the usual high school hijinks and high spirits." Ike tapped the side of his nose. "But don't let his stuffy facade fool you, young lady."

Nathan made a face. "You both make me sound so boring."

She lifted her chin. "Responsible isn't boring."

As a camp counselor, he'd been gentle with the kids. Dashing, handsome. And so reassuringly safe. The exact opposite of her father. Maybe that's what had drawn her to him in the first place.

"Your mother and I weren't the only ones in this family to benefit from the matchmakers's endeavors." Ike threw his son a look. "I recall Aunt Georgie had a hand in bringing you and Deanna together, too."

Stiffening, Nathan unfolded his arms. "If we're done here, I've got someone coming to install the doggy doors for Rascal."

As a further safety measure, they'd decided to modify Ike's bedroom door and the back door.

She surveyed Nathan's pained expression. Anytime his late wife came into the conversation, he became uncomfortable.

Her gaze dropped to the tablet. "I'll make some calls and see what I can arrange so Ike can resume the weekly ROMEO get-togethers."

"Outstanding." Ike slapped his palm on the leather armrest. "Thank you. Can't wait."

She looked at Nathan. "I'd like to take him to the Mason Jar this week, but after I'm gone, arrangements will need to be made for future transportation."

"Right." Nathan sneered. "Lest we forget, your days with us are numbered."

Gemma reared a fraction. "And *after I'm gone*," she reiterated with some heat in her voice, "going forward the situation will need to be continually assessed per Ike's condition."

She was never sure where she stood with Nathan. Whether he would be sorry to see her go, or if he couldn't wait to be rid of her. His inexplicable moods shifted daily. Like the direction of the wind.

"Got it." He straightened. "Now if you'll excuse me…" He padded toward the kitchen to retrieve his boots and hat. Moments later, the back door squeaked open and then shut with a decisive bang.

She jerked.

"I shouldn't have mentioned Deanna." Ike sounded weary.

She gazed at the empty spot in the doorway. "He must miss her so much."

"Grief and guilt are a toxic combination and until my boy deals with both…"

She threw the older man a sharp glance.

Ike ran his hand over his face. "Deanna's death was sudden and unexpected. She was in Boone, visiting friends. A drunk driver…" His chin sank to his chest.

She put her hand to her throat. "How awful. The boys were so young to lose their mother. And for Nathan…"

Imagining the excruciating pain of his loss, she blinked away tears. A service van pulled up outside the house.

The older man blew out a breath. "I love my son dearly, but it remains a sad but true fact he never appreciates anything or anyone as fully as he should until it's too late."

Unsure what he meant, she frowned. The buzz of a power tool whined from the direction of the kitchen.

Leaving him and Rascal watching a game show on television, she retreated to her bedroom to make her calls. Tom Arledge was refreshingly agreeable to helping his cousin ease back into circulation. Tom also gave her the number at the Mason Jar.

By law, restaurants were required to accommodate assistance dogs and their companions, but she'd found over the years it best to give owners a heads-up and talk through any potential issues. Eating establishments were often leery about how service animals might impact their health code ratings or pose a danger to other customers.

However, she met no resistance from Kara MacKenzie, owner of the Jar. Quite the opposite—the woman was extremely enthusiastic and eager to help. Apparently, her father-in-law, a retired fire chief, was a ROMEO, too.

Gemma made arrangements to bring Ike to the Jar for lunch the next day. And she looked forward to getting to know the vivacious Kara better.

Wandering into the hall, she encountered Ike "supervising" Nathan and a handyman. When she shared her news with Ike, he was delighted at the prospect of tomorrow's reunion with his buddies.

The doggy door installation complete, Ike and Rascal escorted the handyman to his vehicle. Avoiding eye contact, Nathan concentrated on putting his tools into a red toolbox.

"Let's see how his first outing goes and then I'll work on enabling Ike and Rascal to join you and the boys at church on Sunday."

No response. *Fine. Be that way.* The emotional whiplash from his mood swings was tiresome. Been there, done that.

Subject to her father's erratic behavior, she'd spent her childhood walking on eggshells. A grown woman, she no longer had to put up with any man's bad attitudes, much less Nathan Crenshaw's.

Miffed, she wheeled, intending to return to her bedroom and answer a few emails from PawPals.

"Gemma, wait."

She halted midstep, but she didn't turn around.

"I have a bad habit of taking out my baggage on those around me."

She faced him.

Contrition darkened his eyes. "I'm sorry. Thank you for everything you're doing to make Dad's life happier." He scoured his face with his hand. "I'm not so great with words, but you've brought life back into this house." His chest heaved. "Into my life, too."

Her heart pounded. "Being here has been a joy. Getting to know the boys…" She took a breath. "Spending time with you."

"Like old times. No. Better." He gave her a lopsided grin that set her heart fluttering. "Gives me hope good times are coming again for all of us."

What those good times would look like, and who they would include, she didn't know. But coming here had set into motion a course of events whose outcome was still undetermined. She understood what he was saying, though. Nothing would ever be the same for her, either.

Her empty apartment, her work and her friends no longer seemed enough.

She felt on the cusp of a turning point. The new start she so desperately yearned for. Would her new start include the man standing before her?

Gemma didn't—couldn't—know the future. But the small treacherous part of herself—that never let go of the man she'd loved and lost—couldn't help breathing a prayer somehow it would.

Chapter Six

Midmorning the next day, she, Ike and Rascal set off in her car for the ROMEO rendezvous at the Mason Jar.

As they drove down Main Street, Ike enthusiastically pointed out various landmarks. It was her first glimpse of the mountain hamlet of which the Crenshaws were so fond.

He insisted on giving her the grand tour so she drove the long way around the town square lined with oak trees. The river bended around the town like a horseshoe. On the horizon, the Blue Ridge surrounded the town, looming in a perpetual smoky mist from which the mountains derived their name.

"May not look like much to a big-city girl like you." The corners of his eyes fanned out in a lifetime of wrinkles. "But it's home to us."

Home.

She got the attraction of Truelove. The slow pace of life. The simplicity and goodness of small things. Big city or country crossroads, no matter its location, home was invariably beautiful.

She parked in one of the spaces in front of the café across from the square.

They stepped inside. A bell jangled above the door. The aroma of fried eggs and the yeasty smell of biscuits floated past her nostrils. The diner was jam-packed.

At the sight of Rascal, conversations momentarily halted,

but she'd made sure he had on his vest identifying him as a service dog. The Truelove grapevine Ike had bragged about and bemoaned in equal measure must have put out the word. Within a millisecond, everyone returned to their own lunch.

She read through the chalked menu on the wall over a pass-through window to the kitchen. Cherry red swivel stools bolted to the floor lined the long counter edged with chrome.

There was a light in Ike's eyes she hadn't witnessed in her short tenure at the ranch. Unlike his son, he relished the company of people. He pointed to a delectable-looking concoction in the display case by the vintage cash register. "Take my word for it. Kara's award-winning apple galette is not to be missed."

Waitresses in jeans and long-sleeved Mason Jar T-shirts scurried from table to table. Booths lined plate-glass windows overlooking Main Street and the town square. A handful of older gentlemen occupied several tables pushed together.

Tom waved them over. She'd briefed Tom to remain alert for signs Ike might be getting tired or overwhelmed. Since it was his first public foray with Rascal, feeling not unlike what she supposed a protective mother might feel, she walked Ike and Rascal to the table.

As she'd advised, to avoid anything remotely triggering that might cause Ike to spiral, Tom went around the table making the introductions. Not only for her benefit but also by way of a reminder for Ike in case his memory failed him.

Nash's family ran the Apple Valley Orchard. Ike clapped him on the back. "As the crow flies, the High Country's closest neighbor in the valley."

She relaxed a smidgen. Ike was having a good day. Fantastic.

Ike slipped into the vacant chair. Rascal plopped at his feet under the table out of the traffic flow. So far so good. Just as she'd trained the sweet collie at PawPals.

Breathing a sigh of relief, she was preparing to make an unobtrusive exit when a pretty, petite blonde touched her elbow.

"Gemma?" The woman, a few years younger, held out her hand. "I'm Kara. I'm so pleased to meet you."

Her gaze cutting to make sure Ike and Rascal were okay, she shook Kara's hand and stepped away to talk with the perky chef.

Kara smiled. "We've never had a service dog visit the Jar before. I don't want to distract Rascal from his job, and per health code regulations I'm not allowed to serve him food, but would it be okay if I provided him a bowl of water?"

Her heart warmed. "Not many people think of the animal. Thank you. He'd love a bowl of water."

"Will you stay for lunch? If I do say so myself, the blue plate special—beef bourguignon—"

She couldn't help but smile at Kara's exquisite French pronunciation.

"On a cold November day like today..." Kara kissed the tips of her fingers. "It's simply *magnifique* if I do say so myself."

Gemma threw another glance at the ROMEOs. "I don't want him to feel like I'm hovering."

Kara drew her away to the farthest booth. "Would this work?"

She nodded. "Thank you."

"Training dementia assistance dogs must be so rewarding. I admire the work you do." Kara's remarkable eyes, a shade resembling blueberries, misted. "Maggie has raved about the difference you've made for Ike."

Gemma slid into the booth. "That's why I do what I do. Hoping to make life better for clients and their families. And I love working with the dogs."

"Would you mind if I joined you for lunch?" Kara lingered. "As one out-of-towner to another, I'd love to get to know you better."

"I'd like that." She gestured to the other side of the booth. "But isn't this your busy time?"

Kara laughed. "Actually, other than overseeing menu planning, I've trained my staff so well, I've nearly worked myself out of a job. Tell me what interests you for lunch and I'll bring it to the table myself."

She chose the hearty French stew. Over coffee, she learned Kara's husband was the local fire chief, a position he'd taken over from his father.

"Sort of like Maggie's husband, Bridger, took over as chief of police from his father-in-law, Tom?"

A former city girl, Kara chuckled. "Small towns."

Gemma had firsthand experience with the quirks of small-town life. Everyone knew everyone else, both its major appeal and its primary downside. Once upon a time, she'd been a small-town girl, too, until she could no longer live in the shadow of what her father had done.

In contrast to her own deeply engrained reticence, Kara was remarkably open about the struggles she'd faced as a child living in homeless shelters until she was adopted after her mother died.

She admired Kara's candor, how comfortable and secure she was with herself and where she came from. She wished she could be more like her. She'd learned over the years to share just enough for the conversation to not feel one-sided. She'd become skillful at diverting questions about her childhood.

The bell at the door jangled. Kara straightened. "Here comes trouble."

Several older women trooped past to a vacant table underneath the community bulletin board.

"I'm guessing the matchmakers?"

Kara rolled her eyes. "I see you've been warned. GeorgeAnne and I had a now-resolved issue over pie versus galette, but she helped Will and I find happiness together."

She peered around Kara. "Which one is Ike's aunt?"

Kara took a quick peek over her shoulder. "GeorgeAnne's the skinny, scary one with her back to the wall. No doubt scoping out her next victim. Just don't let it be you."

Lips twitching, Gemma took a surreptitious second look. Nathan's great-aunt was an angular, faintly terrifying woman with ice-blue eyes and a short, iron gray cap of hair.

"She's the bossy one." Kara made a face. "Although, considering the rest of them, that's probably splitting hairs. The pleasantly plump one is a distant relative of mine, ErmaJean. The tiny one is Miss IdaLee, who taught forty years' worth of Truelove children. On the end is GeorgeAnne's sister, Cora-Faye, a terror in her own right. If you don't believe me, ask her daughter-in-law, Kate Dolan."

The bell clattered again. Kara's gaze sharpened. "But maybe putting your marital destiny in their hands might not be such a bad idea. Not if hunky Nathan Crenshaw is on the market again. What do you say to that?"

Gemma went crimson. "We're colleagues on Ike's care team. I'm not looking for... He's not interested in..." She brought the glass of water to her mouth.

"Oh, it's like that, is it?" A shadow fell over the booth. Kara's gaze lifted. "Good to see you, Nate."

Blue eyes sparking with mischief, the chef threw her a slightly wicked grin. "Why don't you keep Gemma company while I bring her a slice of apple galette and get you some lunch?"

Gemma made a grab for her, but too late. Kara slipped out of the booth.

A perplexed frown creased Nathan's forehead. "Okay..." He took Kara's vacated seat.

"What's your pleasure today?" Kara beamed at them. "Interested in trying something new?" She winked.

Gemma gaped at her.

Nathan, like most men *thank the Lord*, appeared impervious to any subtext in conversation. He shrugged. "Sure. I'll like whatever you pick for me."

She could see the effort it was costing Kara not to respond to that leading remark. She glared at her new, maybe not so good, friend.

Kara smirked. "I'll get right on that." She sauntered toward the swinging door with the porthole, separating the kitchen from the dining area.

When Gemma could no longer stand the tension strung between them like a high wire, she said, "I didn't realize you were coming into town today."

Removing his hat, he laid it on the seat beside him. "I didn't know myself, but with Dad occupied I decided to catch one of the rancher association meetings this morning at the county seat. When I got back, the house felt too empty." His gaze dropped. "I thought I'd have a bite at the Jar."

"And check out how your dad is doing, too?"

"Guilty as charged." He met her gaze. "Sorry."

He wore such a hangdog puppy look, she couldn't help but smile.

"Nothing to be sorry about." She took a sip of water. "I was concerned, too, but he's having a great time. As for Rascal? It's kind of like Graduation Day for him and I'm so proud. How silly a doggy mom am I?"

"You're not silly."

Good thing she was already seated—his dazzling smile might have buckled her knees otherwise.

"Here's your French onion soup."

They jolted. Nathan sat back. She pretended an intense fascination with a packet of artificial sweetener.

Kara put a steaming bowl in front of him and a side plate of crusty French bread. "Enjoy."

She motioned to one of the younger waitresses, who brought

over a glass of water for Nathan and an enormous slice of the most decadent apple dessert Gemma had ever beheld.

Her eyes widened. "I can't eat this by myself, Kara."

"That's why I gave you two forks. Nate probably wouldn't mind helping you out." Kara batted her eyes. "You can thank me later."

Pursing her lips, Gemma leveled a glance at her. Apparently, the Double Name Club wasn't the only Truelove matchmakers. Kara waggled her fingers at them and headed to the kitchen.

Again, thankfully the subtext was lost on Nathan. Saying a brief grace, the rancher dug into his lunch.

When he came up for air, he asked, "Do you have a dog of your own, Gemma?"

She shook her head. "Training assistance dogs doesn't leave much time or energy for a pet." She shrugged. "Maybe one day. Plus, PawPals headquarters is in Laurel Grove, about a thirty-minute drive from my Greensboro apartment."

Fork midway to his mouth, he paused. "That's where you and Juliet grew up. She was a counselor at camp that summer, too. With your best friend and your workplace there, I'm surprised you don't still live in Laurel Grove."

"Guess I'm a big-city girl at heart. It's nearer the airport." She made an effort to relax her shoulders from where they'd bunched near her ears at the mention of her former hometown. "I'm away a lot, acclimating clients to their new service companions. I'd love a dog of my own, but being cooped up in my small apartment wouldn't be fair."

Eager to deflect the conversation away from Laurel Grove, she handed him a fork. "Want to share?"

He smiled. "Thought you'd never ask."

The galette was delicious.

She savored the crisp sweetness of the apples. "Totally lives up to the hype."

Nathan laid down his fork. "I guess this is the first time we've actually eaten a meal out together."

"Hot dogs around the bonfire at the lake surrounded by little campers doesn't exactly qualify, does it?"

Soon as the words left her mouth, she would have done anything to take them back. Anything personal from the past— the elephant in the room—was one of the subjects she took care to avoid with him.

Instead of being annoyed, he laughed. "Company's just as good." He stabbed his fork into the pie again. "But this time around, the food is a lot better."

She became aware of GeorgeAnne, a woman she'd never met, scowling at her from across the diner. Although why, she had no idea.

"I should go." She grabbed her cell off the table. "Maggie invited me to stop by the Hollingsworth kennel. There's a dog she and Bridger wanted me to meet as a possible future candidate for K-9 dementia assistance training. But I'll be back to the ranch soon. Tom is bringing Ike home."

Nathan picked up the bill before she could get it. "Lunch is on me. Don't worry about hurrying back to the ranch. I'm planning on being there all afternoon."

"This has been nice." She hesitated. "I don't want to argue again, but it's important someone is with Ike at all times."

He stilled. "It has been nice. We're going to have to agree to disagree on this issue. Dad will be fine. Enjoy your afternoon off."

She couldn't shake a disquieting feeling of looming disaster on the horizon, but as Nathan had pointed out yesterday, she was merely a dog trainer. "Thank you for lunch."

"See you at home."

Gemma blinked at his choice of words. Either *home* didn't have the same connotation for him as it did for her, or he didn't notice the slip of his tongue.

He cocked his head. "Everything okay?"

A stark longing for everything she'd wanted and had never been fulfilled blazed in her heart. If only things had turned out differently for them... But they hadn't.

She swallowed past the boulder in her throat. "See you soon."

Before she lost what little control she possessed over her ragged emotions, she hurried out. Yet she had the uncomfortable sensation of eyes following her to the exit.

Nathan or GeorgeAnne Allen? Friend or foe?

As much as she hated the conflict with him, she feared friendship might prove more dangerous to her hard-won peace of mind.

Chapter Seven

Nate lingered over his coffee. GeorgeAnne plopped into Gemma's vacated seat. From the look on her face, she had something to say. Given her track record, it didn't take a genius to figure out what.

"Don't start with the matchmaking, Aunt Georgie." He folded his arms across his chest. "Gemma is only in Truelove in a professional capacity."

GeorgeAnne looked at him over the top of her horn-rimmed glasses. "I wouldn't dream of it. The girls and I have already discussed it—"

The "girls" of the Double Name Club would never see seventy again.

"We agree you and Gemma Anderson Spencer or whatever she calls herself these days..." GeorgeAnne waved a bony, imperious hand. "You two wouldn't make a good match."

"Oh, really?" Hackles unaccountably rising, he narrowed his eyes. "And why is that?"

His great-aunt sniffed. "She's not from around here."

In Southern-speak, that meant Gemma didn't and never would belong.

He stiffened. "She's from Greensboro, not the moon."

"She's the emotional equivalent of quicksand, my boy." Leaning forward on her elbows, his great-aunt warmed to her theme. "She's an excellent dog trainer. And she's been extremely compassionate with Ike, but she's a city girl. Not the right kind of woman to be a rancher's wife."

Gemma would make an excellent rancher's wife. Though of course, not his.

"She's unreliable. Capricious in her affections. And secretive."

He frowned. "That's not fair."

GeorgeAnne shook her finger at him. "I haven't forgotten how devastated you were when she broke things off with you without any explanation."

"That was fifteen years ago, Aunt Georgie. She's changed."

"What do you know about her? Her family? Or her background? Did she ever—does she ever—talk about any of that?"

He shook his head.

She raised her voice in triumph. "Exactly."

An unexpected and unwelcome protectiveness for Gemma surged in his chest. "We're both different people."

She gave him a look. "Life has a way of working out for the best. Who knows how your life would've turned out if you'd stuck with her?"

How indeed...

"You certainly wouldn't have enjoyed a rock-solid, thirteen-year marriage to a woman who adored you. Or have two of the most delightful children God ever created." She curled her lip. "You'd probably have ended up in some place like where she's from—"

"Greensboro is hardly the back side of Mars."

"Surrounded by concrete..." GeorgeAnne threw out her hands. "Possibly selling insurance."

He rolled his eyes. "Anything but that."

GeorgeAnne arched her eyebrow. "I thought you'd be pleased with our noninterference pact. You're always accusing the Double Name Club of unwanted meddling. Well, this is us not interfering."

"For once," he huffed.

Then the natural caution that must be exercised when dealing with any of the Double Name Club reasserted itself. "Unless this is some kind of reverse psychology strategy you're trying?"

Her mouth pinched. "I'm crushed you have so little faith in my integrity."

Not buying her affronted sensibilities, he snorted. "You forget I've seen how you operate. The matchmaking shenanigans you've waged against practically everyone I know. Bridger and Maggie. Luke and Shayla. Clay and Kelsey." He jerked his thumb in the direction of the booth where the recipients of the matchmakers' most recent campaign were eating lunch. "Colton and Mollie."

GeorgeAnne gave him what for her passed as a smile. "Successful, happy matches each and every one. You'll find no complaints from any in that quarter."

"Not now, but at the time…"

"Water under the bridge of their eventual domestic bliss." She patted his hand. "Not something you have to worry about."

At his startled look, she squeezed his hand. "No doubt someday when you're ready, you'll find eventual domestic bliss once again." Her mouth thinned. "But not with the K-9 trainer. She's totally unsuitable. You two wouldn't be a good fit. Besides, it's not like she's sticking around. As I understand it, the training ends next week. To which I say, goodbye and good riddance."

He gaped at his great-aunt. "You're serious about not pushing us together, aren't you?"

One for the record books, for the Truelove matchmakers, a match not-in-the-making.

"Absolutely." She eased out of the booth. "You've been through so much losing dear Deanna."

When he returned to Truelove that summer after Gemma

broke his heart, his aunt had been a huge, give-hometown-Deanna-a-chance advocate.

"And you're going through so much with your dad… Ike's always been my favorite nephew."

"You say that about all your nephews," he muttered. "Maggie's dad, Tom, too."

His great-aunt lifted her chin. "You've got enough on your plate without dealing with someone like Gemma." She rose. "Although, if your thoughts are once again contemplating romance… I would urge you to take another look at our local veterinarian. Ingrid is the epitome of stability and levelheadedness."

Ingrid might be great with animals, but with humans not so much, and she certainly wasn't mother material for his sons.

"My boys have a mother," he grunted.

GeorgeAnne's wrinkled face softened. "I'm not trying to be cruel, Nate. Deanna would want her sons looked after properly, and she wouldn't want you to spend the rest of your life alone."

"I'm looking after my sons."

Yet after what he'd overheard yesterday, that wasn't exactly true. And Gemma's return seemed to have stirred something inside him. Made him aware of how isolated and lonely he'd become.

GeorgeAnne scanned his face. "If Ingrid doesn't take your fancy, then someone else. We'll keep a discreet lookout for additional blondes." She threw him a wry look. "A preference of yours." With that parting shot, she exited the diner amid a clatter of jangling bells.

He stared after her.

Instead of taking comfort from her uncharacteristic hands-off pronouncement, he was left with a disquieting sense of alarm.

* * *

It wasn't long after GeorgeAnne left that the ROMEOs got ready to leave, too.

Nate headed over to Tom and his dad with Rascal.

At the cash register, his father fished his wallet out of his pocket, but Tom waved his money away. "I've got it this time, old friend."

Nate's dad thanked him. "How about I leave a tip?"

"Great." Tom handed his credit card to the cashier. He and Nate watched his dad return to the ROMEO table to lay down a few bills. "I'm so pleased to see Ike is more like his old self."

The waitress ran Tom's card through the machine.

Nate nodded. "The changes Gemma has made to his routine and the medication adjustment are doing the trick."

"So many reasons to feel optimistic for him." Tom signed his name to the receipt. "When I take Ike to the ranch, I'll stick around until you or Gemma get back."

"I appreciate that, Tom, but I need to head home and do some bookkeeping. I'll take Dad with me and save you the trip."

The waitress handed Tom his receipt. The retired Truelove police chief folded the slip of paper and squared it away in his wallet. "If you've got work to do, I don't mind sitting with him."

Nate made a face. "You've been talking to Gemma, haven't you?" He paid the waitress for his lunch.

Tom's brow creased. "She's concerned about Ike being left on his own and getting confused."

"Which is why Dad has Rascal. Gemma is being overly cautious. Dad wouldn't appreciate a babysitter."

Tom fingered his chin. "When Gemma and I worked out this arrangement to bring Ike to the weekly ROMEO lunches, she was adamant about not leaving him alone."

Nate furrowed his brow. "Like you said, he's more himself than he's been in months. I'll be in the next room. He'll be fine."

Tom didn't appear convinced. "If you're sure."

Fifteen minutes later, Nate and his father arrived at the ranch. The field trip to the diner had taxed his dad. His father didn't protest when Nate suggested he lie down for a short nap.

Nate sat at the large, antique desk that had been his dad's and his grandfather's before him. The pile of paperwork never seemed to diminish. Maybe he could pay a few bills and put in an online order to pick up tomorrow at the agri-supply store. He'd been working about an hour when he remembered he needed to check on a heifer, calving for the first time next month.

Pushing back from the desk, he soon located the heifer in the pasture with the other cattle. Other than being a mite ornery— he grinned at what Deanna would have said to that—the heifer looked to be doing well.

"Won't be long now." He patted the heifer with affection. Deanna would have said not soon enough. He smiled.

It struck him it was the first time since her death, the thought of her hadn't brought an instant stab of pain. Or guilt.

Gazing over the herd, he pinched the bridge of his nose.

She'd been an excellent mother. A wonderful homemaker and rancher's wife. Their thirteen-year marriage had been strong, mainly because of Deanna.

"I'm sorry," he whispered into the wind. "Did you feel loved enough?"

To his dying day, he'd regret not telling her he loved her more often. On their last day together, he'd wasted it by arguing over something trivial. Then it was too late.

His time with Deanna ran out.

The wind and sorrow whipping at his heels, he was on his way to the house when Gemma's car pulled into the drive.

A yearning rose in his chest. Stealing his breath. Accelerating his heart. The aching vulnerability frightened him. Instead of embracing it, he shoved the feelings aside and allowed irritation to replace them.

She opened the door and got out.

Nate stalked toward the car. "I don't appreciate you talking behind my back with Tom about Dad."

Her smile faded. "Where's Ike?"

"In the house. And don't change the subject." He threw out his hands. "What did you hope to gain by dumping that on Tom? Get him to side with you?"

Her brown eyes darkened. "This isn't about taking sides. This is about keeping your father safe."

Nate rocked on his heels. "I'd never do anything to put my father in jeopardy. His care is my number-one priority."

Arms folded, she got in his face. "And my number-one priority—"

The doggy door flew open. There was a streak of sable-colored fur. Barking furiously, Rascal raced toward them. Clamping his teeth into the sleeve of Nate's jacket, the growling collie tugged hard, nearly knocking him off his feet.

He staggered. "Get this crazy dog off me." He tried to free himself, but the collie's grip was tenacious. "What's wrong with him? Does he think I was threatening you?"

"I don't know what's got into him. I've never seen him like this. He's not an aggressive animal. Rascal," she commanded. "Release."

Ignoring her, the collie continued to forcibly drag Nate across the yard. Resisting, Nate stood his ground. There was a ripping sound. A piece of the fabric from his coat came loose, clenched between Rascal's jaws.

The dog went into a defensive half crouch. Howling, he leaped up and ran in a tight circle around Nate. Rascal barreled into the back of Nate's legs, almost sending him sprawling.

"Rascal!" She tried to pull the dog off him. With a growl, he snapped at her.

She fell against the fence. "I've never had one of my dogs… Wait. Do you smell smoke? Nathan!" Gasping, she pointed. "The house is on fire."

He whirled. Black smoke leaked from around the door-frame. The fire alarm shrieked. He spotted flames through the kitchen window.

The farmhouse was on fire. And inside was his dad.

Nate sprinted toward the house, but Rascal raced ahead.

"Don't go in there," Gemma screamed. "I'm calling the fire department. Wait for help to arrive."

"There's no time," he shouted. "Stay here!"

Rascal leaped through the doggy door and disappeared into the burning house.

Without stopping to think, he reached for the doorknob. Thankfully, it remained cool to the touch. Twisting it, he flung open the door. A cloud of smoke assailed his nostrils.

Coughing, he threw up his arm to cover his nose and mouth. "Dad!" he yelled. "Dad, where are you?"

There was no sign of his father or Rascal. Plunging into the swirling, choking darkness, he spotted flames licking at what was left of a pot on the stovetop.

He seized the hand towel they always left draped over the drainboard. With it, he grabbed hold of the pot handle and flung it into the stainless-steel sink. He turned off the stove and turned the faucet full blast onto the contents of the pot. Hissing, steam rose. He sputtered.

From the living room, there came a frenzy of barking. Stumbling out of the kitchen, he found his father crouched behind his recliner with his hands over his ears. Rascal nudged his dad, trying to get him to move.

The alarm continued its deafening shriek.

His father's eyes were wild and frightened. "Make it stop…" His chin trembled.

It struck Nate like a blow to the chest how much he resembled Kody—childlike and utterly dependent. A complete role reversal.

He pulled his father upright. "Let's get you someplace safe."

Bewildered, his father allowed himself to be towed out of the living room. Gemma met them in the kitchen. She'd flung open the window and, using the towel he'd abandoned, she was trying to clear the air by fanning away the fumes and smoke.

His heart contracted. "Gemma!"

She took his dad's other arm, and they propelled him out of the kitchen and into the yard. His father dropped onto the brown, winter-withered grass.

A siren blared. His dad cringed. Talking to his father in a low, soothing voice, Gemma sat down and put her arm around him.

His heart thudded. He found it difficult to draw an even breath. Bending double, he propped his hands on his thighs. Whining softly, Rascal rubbed his face along his leg.

"If you hadn't come to get me, Rascal…" His voice hitched. "Good boy. Such a good boy." He ran his hand over the collie's coat. If he hadn't been able to reach his father in time, he had no doubt Rascal would have remained with his dad, a faithful, loyal companion to the very end.

Rumbling up the drive, an engine with the Truelove Volunteer Fire Department rolled to a shuddering stop. Friends and neighbors in turnout gear jumped out of the fire truck. Behind the engine, an ambulance screamed to a halt. Luke Morgan and Zach Stone exited the vehicle at a run.

Fire Chief Will MacKenzie dashed over to him. "The boys!"

"Still at school," he rasped. *Thank You, God.* His nose and his eyes burned. His throat felt raw.

What if the boys had been in the house? What if the fire

had gotten out of control before he arrived? If he'd been in the back pasture, he would have never heard the alarm.

A wave of dizziness overcome him. He swayed and would have hit the ground hard if Will's second-in-command, Lieutenant Bradley, hadn't caught hold of him and eased him to a sitting position.

"The fire's out," Nate wheezed. "A pot was left on the stove."

"My men will do a thorough assessment to be sure." The chief sent Bradley and several other firefighters into the house. Seconds later, the screech of the fire alarm went silent.

Will motioned EMTs Luke and Zach forward. "Nate needs to be checked out."

Nate shoved at the oxygen mask Zach tried to fit over his face. "I'm fine."

The young owner of the Truelove auto body shop wasn't so easily deterred. "Smoke inhalation isn't anything to play with. Take a few deep breaths and let us check you out."

Luke fitted a mask over his dad's nose and mouth. He figured his father would fight Luke, but in his current state of befuddlement, the older man offered no resistance.

Will hovered over Gemma. "Ma'am?"

She fluttered her hand. "I'm fine." Patches of black soot streaked across her high cheekbones. "I wasn't in there long."

Nate ripped the mask from his mouth. "You shouldn't have been in there at all." Black spots danced before his eyes. "I told you to stay outside."

Her lips quivered. "You might've needed my help."

"You might've gotten yourself killed," he growled. The notion of what could have happened to her—to all of them—was like a punch to the gut. Fear and nausea roiled in his belly.

The chief moved away for a consultation with his men and then returned. Will pushed his helmet back on his head. "The fire was contained to the range. The damage was minimal, but the stovetop's a total loss. It'll need to be replaced. But at least we didn't have to go in there with the hoses. Water damage is a whole other kettle of fish."

A distant cousin—one of GeorgeAnne's sons who ran the family hardware store—stepped forward. "I've put in a call to my wife. She's bringing a dehumidifier. That will help a lot. Mom said to tell you not to fret. She and the family will be here ASAP to do a deep cleaning."

Nate shook his head. "I appreciate that, but it's only the kitchen. I can handle—"

"Family helps family." His cousin, closer to Nate's father's age than his own, removed his helmet and held it under his arm. "Smoke penetrates an entire house. All surfaces need to be disinfected with baking soda. Charcoal will help absorb much of the smell. The curtain, rugs, and upholstery must be vacuumed with a special HEPA filter. Clothing and bedding also run through a wash cycle of vinegar."

Nate gaped at him.

Will grimaced. "It looked like something was left too long on the burner."

His dad yanked off the oxygen mask. "I wanted to surprise everyone by fixing your mom's soup. I'm getting a little forgetful." He peered at his Allen cousin. "Who are you again? I know I should remember."

Nate winced. His father and Brian Allen had known one another their entire lives. But Brian's expression never wavered. There was only compassion in his hazel eyes.

Kneeling beside Nate's father, he put his hand on the older man's shoulder. "It's Brian, GeorgeAnne's oldest. Mom will be here soon. She'll soon have you set to rights."

"Brian?" The confusion cleared from his dad's face. "I knew that. Sometimes I just need a reminder."

Sadness engulfed Nate.

Will removed his gloves. "Didn't you smell something burning?"

Nate pinched the bridge of his nose. "Dad was taking a nap. I'd stepped out to check on a heifer."

"It took a while for the liquid in the soup to burn through the pot." Will's gaze cut between him and his father. "How long were you away from the house?"

Guilt smote Nate. "I only meant to be gone a few moments, but time got away from me."

"I don't mean to add to your troubles, but if you understood how quickly things can go wrong... If you saw the things we see on a weekly basis..." The fire chief scrubbed his hand over his face. "This could've easily turned into a tragedy today."

Nate got to his feet. "I know," he whispered. "I'm sorry."

Standing at his side, Gemma slipped her hand into his. At her gesture of support, he blinked away the treacherous moisture in his eyes.

Will's dark brown eyes pinned him in place. "Perhaps it would be best if Ike was no longer left on his own."

Nate looked at Gemma and then at the fire chief. "I see that now. It won't happen again."

Will gave him a short, decisive nod. He shouted an order to one of his men. "We'll get out of your way and head to the station."

Nate thrust out his hand. "Thank you." The fire chief shook his hand.

"Don't hesitate to call whenever you need us." Will touched the rim of his helmet. "Ma'am. Mr. Ike, sir."

Nate nudged his chin at Luke and Zach. "Thank you, guys."

"Your dad inhaled more smoke than you did." Luke reslung the stethoscope around his neck. "It would make me feel better if you got him checked out at the ER. Better safe than sorry."

"I'll do that."

The EMTs and firefighters packed their gear and departed.

He took out his phone. "I should let Maggie know what's happened. It might be better for the boys to have a sleepover tonight with Austin and Logan."

A caravan of vehicles approached, including GeorgeAnne's GMC pickup.

His father rose. "Reinforcements have arrived." Waving, he and Rascal moved to greet them.

Nate stared after his dad. "It's like the fire never happened. Much less that he started it."

He raked his hand through his hair, only just realizing his head was bare.

She handed him his hat. "It fell off when you bolted toward the house. I kept it safe for you."

"You were right about not leaving Dad alone." He sighed. "I thought I'd accepted the truth about the inevitable, worsening nature of his condition, but I've been in denial."

"There's no blueprint for navigating the emotional fallout for this illness."

"It's going to be a long goodbye, isn't it?" He swallowed. "Losing him, one inch at a time. A thousand little deaths."

She gazed after his dad, chatting with GeorgeAnne and her daughters-in-law. "I hate this disease for what it does, not only to the patient but their families, too."

He pursed his lips. "Once I get GeorgeAnne started in the kitchen, I'll take Dad to the ER."

"Please let me come." She touched his arm. "I won't be able to rest until I know Ike is really okay."

From across the yard, he was aware of GeorgeAnne's stern gaze burning a hole through him.

Broadening his chest, he placed his hand over Gemma's. "Thank you. Your wisdom and company would be most appreciated."

At the hospital, he and Gemma waited in the reception area while his father's doctor, called in by the attending ER physician, did a complete assessment. The doctor had also supplied a list of agencies that provided daily in-home care services. Nate managed to call through the list before business hours ended for the day.

After talking to the last agency on the list and feeling hopeless, he clicked off his cell.

"Bad news?"

"With the holidays approaching, their care providers are already booked with other clients. The lady said she couldn't make any promises, but she hoped someone might be available after New Year's Day." He sighed. "What am I going to do about Dad until then?"

"You're going to let me be there for Ike until you can secure a full-time caregiver."

He looked at her. "I couldn't ask you to do that."

"You're not asking. I'm offering." She squared her shoulders. "As for any concerns you might have, I have an LPN license. I worked at a memory care facility for four years after high school before I joined PawPals and got into K-9 training."

He shook his head. "But this would require a five-week commitment."

"I won't start training the next dog until the third week in January. I'm totally free to look after your dad." She steepled her hands under her chin. "Please. Let me do this for you, for Ike, for Connor and Kody."

He looked at her. Truly looked at her. His great-aunt was wrong. She had changed from the young girl who broke his heart without so much as an explanation, much less an apology.

Unless that's what this was—a misguided attempt at redemption?

He cleared his throat. "You don't have to make up for what happened in the past."

She blinked. "That's not what this is. I care about Ike. I care how his illness impacts Connor and Kody. I can understand how you might not believe me, but I care about you, too." She half turned away from him. "I always have," she whispered.

His heart jolted. Was that true? If it was, it completely altered the lens through which he'd viewed that long-ago summer. And perhaps also his perspective on the future.

"Of course, maybe you can't wait for me to get out of your life." She lowered her gaze. "I don't blame you if you never want to see me again."

Never see her again… His gut clenched. "If you're sure about taking care of Dad for the duration of the holidays…"

"I'm sure."

He took a ragged breath. "Thank you."

An odd sense of relief filled him. Her staying in Truelove felt like a reprieve of sorts. Five weeks… He hadn't been ready to say goodbye.

He was beginning to wonder if he ever would.

Chapter Eight

Over the next few days, GeorgeAnne and her crew did an amazing job restoring the farmhouse to livable conditions.

Yet with so many extra people in the house, Ike was feeling out of his routine. Gemma had her hands full with him, but she pitched in with the Truelove contingent whenever she could.

She also made time each day to call Connor and Kody who were on an extended sleepover at Maggie's. Her little guys were understandably distraught about their temporary exile from the only home they'd ever known.

Her little guys?

They weren't her little guys. But it felt as if they were. They'd become so dear to her.

She called her friend and PawPals boss, Juliet, to let her know about her decision to stay in Truelove a while longer.

Her announcement was met with a long beat of silence. Then Juliet asked, "Is this the right thing to do in this situation, Gem?"

She frowned into the cell phone in her hand. "Ike needs care. The agency can't provide anyone until after the New Year."

"I meant the right thing for you."

Sitting on the bed in the guest bedroom, she tucked a loose tendril of hair behind her ear. "Ike needs my help."

"You mean it's Nathan who needs your help."

She stiffened. "What if he does?"

"Considering how you feel about him, I'm not sure staying on another month is a good idea."

"Nathan and I are friends, Juliet." She clenched the phone. "Friends help friends."

"We both know that isn't what's going on here. This is about your unresolved feelings for him. What is it you're hoping to achieve by sticking around?"

She got off the bed. "Ike—"

"I'm talking about you, Gemma. Is something more than friendship growing between you?"

If only... The longing was so sharp, she bit her lip to stem the flow of it. "He's grieving his wife. And grappling with the anticipatory grief of what's happening to his father."

"Then what possible good will come from prolonging the agony of being there with him but not *with* him in any meaningful sense?" Juliet prodded. "I know a thing or two about grief, remember?"

Juliet lost her first husband, a soldier, to combat. Gemma had watched helpless from the sidelines as her dear friend nearly went under from the sheer intensity of her loss. Her complicated grieving had almost cost her a chance at a new life with wonderful Rob and his little girl, Sophie.

Gemma gritted her teeth. "If it's in my power to help them, don't you think I should?"

Juliet sighed. "I don't want to see you get hurt. Again. Last time, it was me and the Spencers who picked up the pieces."

Her memories of those first few weeks after her mother's death were hazy at best. The Spencer family had taken her in so she could finish her last year of high school in Laurel Grove.

Restless, she paced beside the bed. "I'm trying to do a good thing, Jules. I like it here. Connor and Kody are wonderful. Everyone has been so kind."

With the exception of Nathan's great-aunt GeorgeAnne. Coordinating restoration efforts over the weekend, the older woman had been a near-constant presence. More than once, she'd felt the older woman's steely, measuring gaze upon her.

"Please be careful, Gem. Don't forget there are people who love you here in Laurel Grove."

From the window, she spotted a blue sedan approaching the farmhouse. "I need to go."

Kara got out of the sedan with a large cardboard box.

Opening the bedroom door, Gemma walked into the hall. "Talk to you soon, Jules. Bye." She clicked off.

In the kitchen, a beehive of activity, she met up with Kara, delivering a week's worth of precooked, gourmet meals to tide them over. They smelled delicious.

"This is so thoughtful of you. Thank you." Making room in the refrigerator for the covered aluminum trays, she could feel the ever-watchful GeorgeAnne glowering at her back.

She wasn't sure what she'd done to earn the Double Name Club member's disfavor, but disapproval was writ large across the woman's rigid features.

Gemma walked Kara out to her car.

Then summoning her courage, she went into the house again. Most people liked her. Animals certainly did. Unwilling to admit defeat, she made one last attempt to draw the older woman out in friendly conversation.

She found GeorgeAnne with Ike and Rascal in the laundry room, pulling bedsheets from the dryer.

"With the stove out of commission, it was so nice of Kara to bring ready-to-heat meals." Gemma grabbed the other end of the flat sheet in the older woman's hands to help fold it. "Everyone has been so kind."

"We care for our own." The sheet strung between them, GeorgeAnne brought her ends together. Gemma did the same. "There are a lot of people who care about this family."

Stepping forward, Gemma met the older woman in the middle with her folded half of the bedsheet. "Including me."

She locked eyes with the Ike's aunt. Something akin to respect stirred in GeorgeAnne's gaze. She figured few people stood up to the indomitable force of nature.

"I appreciate everything you're doing for Ike." The older woman took possession of the sheet. "I just don't want to see a repeat of what happened the last time you came into my great-nephew's life."

"I never meant to—"

"But you did."

Gemma bit her lip.

"Nothing to say for yourself? Even a poor excuse is better than none."

Ike's eyes went deer-in-the-headlights. "Georgie…"

Gemma swallowed. "I'm sorry, Miss GeorgeAnne."

The Double Name Club member sniffed. "It's not me you should be apologizing to." Pressing her lips together, the older woman stalked away.

Nathan's dad put his arm around Gemma. Rascal licked her hand. "My aunt is a funny old bird. Protective of her family. Deanna was a particular favorite of hers."

"I hope I haven't given the impression I'm trying to take Deanna's place…" She went crimson. "You don't think I'm trying to replace Deanna in the boys' affections, do you?"

"Absolutely not. You have your own place in our affections."

But what about Nathan? Maybe it was hard for him to see another woman fixing meals in Deanna's kitchen…spending time with Deanna's sons…occupying space that by rights belonged to Deanna, never her.

Ike rubbed his hand over his face. "Have you talked with Nate about what happened that summer?"

She wrapped her arms around herself. "I think it's a topic best avoided."

Ike shook his head. "All these years, he's struggled to make sense of why you broke things off with him. All I'm saying is, it would mean more than you can imagine to Nate if you would talk to him about your reasons. It'd bring both of you closure if nothing else."

"I'm not sure I can," she rasped.

He rested his hand on Rascal's head. "Just think about it. That's all I'm asking." He shuffled out of the laundry room. Rascal padded after him.

Closure. An ending. Was that what Nathan wanted from her? Was that what she wanted?

Her eyes cut to the window overlooking the barnyard. Under the shelter of the lean-to, he'd spent a good part of the day changing the oil in various farm machinery. She wished she knew what he was thinking, but he was a man of few words. The endearing shyness of the boy had turned into a man with nearly impenetrable reserve.

Gemma's offer to stick around and help Nathan care for Ike had been spur-of-the-moment. But perhaps it hadn't been as out of the blue as she wanted to believe.

Truth was, she'd leaped at the chance to extend her stay. She had nothing and no one waiting at her cold, empty apartment. She was in no hurry to leave Truelove, the ranch or... Her heart pounded. Or Nathan.

She wended her way toward the lean-to.

Nathan lifted his head from the guts of the machinery. "Everything okay inside?"

"Almost done with the cleanup."

He wiped his hands on an old oil rag. "Is Dad all right?"

"In his element."

Nathan grinned. "The more the merrier with him."

Something pinged in her chest, momentarily stealing her breath. Ike—and GeorgeAnne—were right. They needed to talk about what happened. But as she recalled the terrible day she returned from camp, the words lodged in her throat.

He cocked his head. "Was there something you needed?

Aunt Georgie sent me out here to do what I needed to do on the farm."

Given the older woman's attitude, she suspected it was a ploy to put as much distance as possible between the two of them. She wasn't sure what his great-aunt was so afraid of. She'd thrown away any chance for something more with him long ago. Their friendship was far more than she had any reason to expect, and she was grateful. So thankful to have even a small space in his life.

"Thankful," she murmured.

He stuck his hands in the pockets of his jeans. "Hard to believe next week's Thanksgiving."

"Thanksgiving?"

"Surely you've heard of Thanksgiving?" Raising his eyebrows, he gave her a crooked grin. "The holiday involving turkey and giving thanks to God for our blessings?"

She rolled her eyes. "I know what Thanksgiving is. It's just this year the holiday's kind of caught me by surprise."

He crimped the rim of his hat and settled it back on his head. "I don't expect you to work through the holiday. You probably have long-standing Thanksgiving plans."

Since she'd joined the team at PawPals, her usual plan had consisted of Juliet strong-arming her into joining the Melbournes for lunch and spending the rest of her day catching up on paperwork.

"I hadn't given Thanksgiving more than a fleeting thought." She'd be welcome at Juliet's. But driving all that way for only one day…

"The boys and Dad would love for you to celebrate with us." He cleared his throat. "*I* would love for you to celebrate with us."

"I'd love that, too." Her gaze locked onto his. "Thank you for inviting me."

"Great." He smiled. "Although, I warn you it's not a traditional Thanksgiving."

"What do you mean?"

"Neither Dad nor I lay claim to any real culinary talent. In the last couple of years, we merely slap a few steaks on the grill." He sighed. "Good thing, I guess, since this year we don't have a stove."

"About that…" She rubbed her mouth. "Brian said to tell you the new oven would be delivered first thing Tuesday."

Nathan and one of Brian's teenage sons had pulled the old, ruined one out from the wall yesterday. Brian had loaded the oven onto his truck and hauled it away.

"Don't worry about the food. Let me cook Thanksgiving dinner for you."

She couldn't believe she'd said that. From Nathan's expression, he appeared just as surprised.

"I didn't invite you to Thanksgiving so you'd cook for us."

She nodded. "I know, but I'd like to." Equally shocking, she discovered she truly wanted to make it a real Thanksgiving for them.

"That's awfully good of you, but your company is more than enough."

"You're sharing your home and family with me. Cooking is the least I can do." She touched his sleeve. "Please let me do this. Turkey and all the fixings." Had she overstepped? "Unless it would bring sad memories."

He looked at her. "Deanna had many wonderful qualities, but traditional she was not. One year, she served Korean barbecue." He shrugged. "Dad and I haven't had a traditional turkey dinner since my mother died. We'd love it. Thank you."

She steepled her hands under her chin. "I can't wait to get started."

"I hope you still feel as enthusiastic four hours into prep. Consider me your sous chef."

She laughed.

"What?"

"Just picturing you in a chef's hat and not a Stetson."

Crossing his arms, he grinned. "I may not be professionally trained like Kara, or Maddie Lovett at the bakery, but I can hold my own."

"Of that I have no doubt."

Late Monday afternoon, Bridger dropped off the boys with take-out bags for dinner. An aroma of French fries wafted through the air.

The boys hadn't been home since the fire. She could tell they were hesitant about what they might find, but the kitchen had been restored to its original state, minus the oven.

"Looks pwetty much the same." Pushing his way past his brother, Kody released a huge sigh of relief. "Let's eat."

Connor tugged at her sweater. "I missed you, Miss Gemma."

Her heart turned over. "I missed you, too, Connor." She hugged him. He smelled of cinnamon spice. And everything nice. Maggie must have been baking.

Nathan ruffled Connor's hair. "What about me and old Granddad? What are we, chopped beef?"

Ike snorted. "Who are you calling old?"

Kody held up the white take-out bag from the Burger Depot. "We bwought the beef."

After dinner, the boys headed out to check on the rabbits.

Finding herself alone with Nathan, she grabbed a pad of paper and a pen from the catch-all drawer next to the refrigerator. "Besides turkey, what says Thanksgiving to you?"

"Pumpkin pie." He leaned his elbow on the counter. "Or pecan. You pick."

The back door squeaked open. Connor and Kody tromped inside.

"Boots!" she and Nathan cried in unison. They smiled at each other.

The boys toed out of their barn boots.

"Watcha doin', Miss Gemma?"

"You've got homework, too, Miss Gemma?"

She tapped the pen against the pad. "I'm taking orders for our Thanksgiving menu."

Kody's eyes got big. "You're gonna be with us on Thanksgiving?"

"If that would be okay with you?"

"Woo-hoo!" Kody fist-pumped the air and did a little dance in his stocking feet around the kitchen island.

Connor didn't say anything, but the smile on his face told her he was also pleased. Unlike his party-waiting-to-happen younger sibling, he was quieter. It was far too easy for most people to overlook Nathan's oldest child. But not on her watch.

She brushed a lock of hair out of his eyes. "What says Thanksgiving to you, honey?"

"Mashed potatoes." His eyes shone. "And gravy. Lots of gravy."

She wrote it down with a flourish. Mashed potatoes she could do, although the gravy would be unexplored territory. She turned toward Kody. "And you, Sir Dances-a-lot?"

He giggled. "Sweet tea."

She wrote it down. "The sweetest."

"And biscuits with butter."

"You got it." She crossed the *t* and dotted the *i*.

He held up his index finger. "One more thing."

Nathan grabbed his youngest and put him in a headlock. "Seriously, Kode? She's not running a cafeteria here."

She waved the pencil. "What else, sweetie?"

Kody freed himself from his father's hold. "Deviled eggs."

Connor snorted. "Deviled eggs for Thanksgiving?"

"Deviled eggs are appropriate for any season, any occasion." She nodded. "Deviled eggs it is."

With Rascal at his heels, Ike ambled into the kitchen. "What's with the hootin' and hollerin'?"

Connor took his grandfather's hand. "Gemma's making Thanksgiving dinner."

Ike grinned. "Is she now?"

"And she's taking pwayer wequests," Kody piped.

Connor planted his hands on his jeans. "Menu requests, Kode. Not prayer requests."

"You pway your way, and I'll pway mine." Kody rubbed his flat little belly. "This is a dweam come true."

Connor snickered. "He's so silly, Miss Gemma."

"The silliest," she agreed.

She and Nathan exchanged a smile.

Ike cleared his throat.

Her cheeks heating, she returned to the matter at hand. "What says Thanksgiving to you, Ike?"

"Cranberry sauce. Green bean casserole." Ike ticked the items off on his fingers. "Sweet potato casserole and apple-cornbread dressing, Nathan's mom's specialty." He cocked his head. "You know what dressing is, don't you?"

She patted his arm. "I may not be from Truelove, but Greensboro is still the South. In coastal, Piedmont or mountain North Carolina—dressing is served alongside the turkey. Not in it."

Ike gestured toward the cupboard over the coffeemaker. "All Pammie's recipes are in there."

"Dad." Nathan opened his hands. "Let's not overwhelm Gemma."

She opened the cabinet. "The recipes are much appreciated." A small wooden box sat on the top shelf.

Nathan reached up and handed it to her. "You do not have to fix all this food."

"It'll be fun." She took the recipe box from him. "I'll make out my shopping list for ingredients."

He scratched his head. "What says Thanksgiving to you?"

She looked away. "Thanksgiving was never a big deal with my family."

He frowned. "But surely you have a favorite."

Corn pudding—Gemma's mom had made the dish every year for Thanksgiving. Until she died. But corn pudding—like most things associated with her family—was best left in the past. The only legacy they'd passed on was shame.

She forced a smile. "It will give me a great deal of joy to make everyone's favorites."

On Tuesday morning with the boys off for their final day of school before the holiday, Nathan hung around the house longer than usual to oversee the delivery and installation of the new stove. Sheepish about the trouble he'd put them to, Ike banned himself from any more cooking.

Gemma spent most of the day combing through Pamela Crenshaw's old recipe box. Inside was a treasure trove. A time capsule from the mid-twentieth century. A family legacy of pleasant, shared gatherings.

She thumbed through the contents. "What was with the obsession with gelatin?"

Lime. Cherry. Orange. Side dish or dessert. There was even a banana loaf recipe which called for gelatin. Blue ink faded, the index cards were splotched and fraying. Some of the oft-listed ingredients she'd never heard of before—like oleo?

It was only after she made her grocery list and planned out when everything had to go into the oven the enormity of the task hit her. And only two days to prepare before the main event.

What had she been thinking? Her skills extended beyond boiling water and the microwave, but this was well out of her comfort zone.

She'd never cooked a turkey in her life. She rested her head in her hands. This had the makings of a culinary disaster. She was doomed.

Perhaps she ought to bow out now, make her excuses and order Thanksgiving takeout from the actual cafeteria in Asheville. But she couldn't bear to disappoint the boys. And by boys she meant Ike and Nathan, too. She'd seen the wistful expression on Nathan's face when his father mentioned the apple-cornbread dressing.

This was no time for pride. She called Maggie.

"Hey, Gemma. How's—"

"What in the world is oleo?" She burst into tears.

After Maggie talked her off the ledge, she gave her new friend a rundown of the corner she'd painted herself into.

"No need to panic, Gemma."

"I wanted this to be a perfect Thanksgiving for Ike. And I still don't know what oleo is," she wailed.

"Oleo is what my grandma called margarine. No matter what you do or don't fix, it'll be perfect because Ike, Nathan and the boys will know how much you care about them. We'll work on this together."

"You must have food preparations to make for your own family."

"Bridger's sister is hosting this year in Fayetteville, where her husband is stationed. I'm bringing an already made pie. We'll head there on Thursday morning so tomorrow I'm totally yours."

"Your sons will be home for the holiday and—"

"Bridger and the boys have plans to work with the new puppies. I'm free to help."

She drew her first even breath in an hour. Maybe this wouldn't be so terrible after all. "If you're sure…"

"This is what friends are for, Gemma. I'm touched you trusted me enough to reach out."

She and Maggie quickly made plans to meet at the Hollingsworth house after Gemma made her grocery run Wednesday morning.

"Oh," Maggie threw in. "Bring enough clean dishes so we can put everything together."

Feeling much better than she had before calling, she thanked her friend again before saying goodbye.

Now Gemma needed to let her oldest friend know she wouldn't be spending Thanksgiving with Juliet's family. But how would Jules take the news?

With some trepidation, she sent a text. Immediately, squiggly dots appeared.

Juliet: Everything going well?

Gemma: I'm cooking Thanksgiving dinner for them.

More dots followed. Including wide-eyed-amazement emojis. Breathing a sigh of relief their friendship remained intact, she chuckled.

Juliet: I want the juicy details re. you & Nathan.

She shook her head. Keeping it professional. Nathan & I r friends.

Juliet: Don't believe you. Have fun with your "friend," We'll miss you.

She smiled. Miss you, too. Happy Thanksgiving.

Just because Juliet got her second chance, happily-ever-after didn't mean she wanted one, too.

Yet despite her oft-stated resistance to romance, when she fell asleep that night, Nathan's handsome features were the last image in her mind.

Chapter Nine

The next morning, with so many tasks on her to-do list, Gemma bounded out of bed. Despite the boys being out of school for the holiday—or perhaps because—the morning was unusually hectic.

When Tom Arledge picked up Ike and Rascal for a pre-Thanksgiving ROMEO get-together, she grabbed her purse to run errands.

Driving away from the ranch, she patted her purse with the all-important shopping list on the seat beside her. She couldn't remember the last time she'd looked forward to a holiday as much.

Holidays had brought out the worst in her father. He nursed his anger and a bottle of liquor, and the combination was a toxic brew. Too often, she and her mother had been the collateral damage.

She hadn't been much older than Kody when she learned to stay well out of his reach. Thanksgiving or Christmas were at best days to endure, never to enjoy.

The first year after she went to live with the Spencers, she'd been too shell-shocked to do much more than go through the motions. Later once their grandkids were born, the Spencers took to spending the holidays out of state. Despite their well-intentioned invitations to go with them, every year she politely declined.

Her excuse—she couldn't leave her current dog-in-progress over the holiday. But the truth was, even with only a canine for company, she never felt as alone as when she found herself surrounded by other people's families.

Leaving the ranch, she stopped at a large grocery chain on the highway outside of Truelove to purchase the items she'd need for Thanksgiving dinner. The store was filled with last-minute shoppers. Holiday music played on the intercom.

Consulting her list, she went aisle by aisle until she had all the ingredients for the most wonderful Thanksgiving ever. Including a few items she hadn't intended to buy.

After going through the checkout, she loaded the bags into her car. The wind was brisk coming off the mountain today. Brown leaves swirled on the pavement underneath her feet.

Returning to Truelove, she found herself humming a Christmas carol. Most of the storefronts were shuttered, except for the Jar, which was doing a booming business.

Per Maggie's instructions, she pulled into the Hollingsworths' driveway and steered around to the back of the house.

To her surprise, a bevy of other vehicles were already parked there, including the GMC pickup she recognized as belonging to Nathan's great-aunt, GeorgeAnne. Her anxiety ratcheted.

Had she misunderstood? Had she gotten the time wrong? Was she interrupting a private party?

Stomach knotting, she threw the car in Reverse, but Maggie dashed out of the house. "Gemma, wait."

Heat flooded her cheeks. She'd been spotted. Any hope of making a graceful, unobtrusive withdrawal faded. Cutting the engine, she got halfway out of the car. Best to make her excuses and beat a hasty retreat.

"You're busy," she called. "No worries." Although, how she was going to pull this dinner off alone threatened to bring on another round of tears.

"Where're you going?" Maggie motioned. "Come inside."

A handful of women filed out of the house. With the exception of GeorgeAnne, the rest of them were around her own age. Like Kara. Maggie introduced her to most of them when they came to help the Crenshaws after the fire.

She wrung her hands. "I... I don't want to intrude."

"You're not intruding." Maggie's ponytail whipped in the breeze. "Everyone is here for you."

She frowned. "For me?"

"Many hands make light work." Maggie smiled. "When I told Aunt Georgie what you were trying to do for Ike and his family, she rallied the troops."

"But everyone has their own dinners to prepare."

Kara stepped forward. "The MacKenzie clan is having Thanksgiving with the Ferguson brood. My mom and sisters-in-law insisted I take a vacation from cooking." Her adoptive mom was the undisputed queen of North Carolina barbecue.

Gemma bit her lip. "You're not taking off if you're helping me."

Maggie smiled. "Kara isn't here in a chef capacity, but as a teacher."

GeorgeAnne harrumphed. "My role is supervisory."

Maggie exchanged a wry look with the others. "Of course it is, Aunt Georgie. Supervising is what you do best."

GeorgeAnne pushed her glasses higher on the bridge of her nose. "We wanted to show our appreciation for everything you're doing to make this holiday season special for Ike and the boys."

"It really is my pleasure." She slumped. "I just got in over my head with the cooking."

"We've got you covered," Callie McAbee, ROMEO Nash's daughter, assured her. The Apple Valley orchard was next door to the ranch.

"Fact is," AnnaBeth, Truelove's resident style maven and

host of the popular weekly podcast *Heart's Home*, interjected. "In our families, we're the second-string cooks. The heavy lifting is done by the older generation. Our only responsibility is to bring a dish or two."

"Life always comes full circle." GeorgeAnne's thin lips creased. "Your generation's turn will come soon enough. Then it will be your responsibility to carry forward the family traditions you learned from your mothers, aunts and grandmothers."

"We brought ingredients to make our own dishes." Lila Gibson, resident landscape artist at nearby Ashmont College, touched Gemma's arm. "No one wanted to miss the chance to help you, have a good time with friends and learn from the best."

"That would be Kara," Kelsey Summerfield declared.

Everyone laughed.

Recently engaged to Bar None ranch owner Clay McKendry, Kelsey co-owned a wedding venue with the petite blond chef, who had fingers in many culinary business pies in Truelove.

Despite her initial misgivings, Gemma found herself and her bags of groceries hauled into Maggie's kitchen.

True to form, GeorgeAnne soon had the medium-sized kitchen and its young cooks organized. Gemma found herself mixing ingredients for a sweet potato casserole with Anna-Beth. Followed by a green bean casserole with Callie. Once assembled, everyone's dishes were labeled and stored in Maggie's garage fridge to be taken home later and put into the oven the morning of Thanksgiving.

Kara gave detailed instructions on how to thaw, prepare and roast a turkey. Gemma took copious notes. Because gravy could be tricky, under Kara's close supervision, she also learned to make a roux to thicken the sauce.

Usually, she didn't feel at ease with people she didn't know. But somehow—thanks to Maggie's hospitality—in the process of cooking alongside each other, Maggie's friends had become her friends, too. The feeling of belonging was new to her and heartwarming. Filling her with no small sense of gratitude.

"If you have time…" She pulled out the worn recipe card from her purse. "There's one more thing Ike specially requested."

Behind the glasses frames, GeorgeAnne's glacier-blue eyes widened. "Is that Pamela Crenshaw's apple-cornbread dressing recipe? I recognize the handwriting."

"It is. This is the one I want to make sure I get right." Maggie took the card from her. "This recipe is a family legend."

"I'm delighted you found it." GeorgeAnne put a liver-spotted hand to her throat. "After she died, I feared it was lost for good."

Callie peered over Kara's shoulder. "I wouldn't mind learning Miss Pamela's recipe, too. After all, apples are kind of a McAbee thing."

Everyone laughed, but declared themselves equally eager to learn.

By two o'clock, Maggie's kitchen smelled amazing. The tantalizing aroma of roasted nuts filled the air. Everyone made short work of helping Maggie put her kitchen to rights.

Her arms full of containers collected from the garage fridge, Kelsey turned to go. "I can't think when I've had so much fun."

"Me, too." Lila was right behind her. "Happy Thanksgiving, everybody."

Callie was next to depart.

"Have you thought about table decor?" On her way out the door, AnnaBeth paused. "Dressing the table is as pleasing to the eye as the food is to the stomach."

"No… I haven't…" She threw Maggie a panicked look.

But it was GeorgeAnne to the rescue. "Deanna kept special holiday decor in the sideboard in the dining room." Nathan's great-aunt tapped her chin. "Knowing my nephew, it's probably right where she left it."

Kara and Maggie insisted on helping Gemma load her car. Walking out with them, GeorgeAnne supervised, per her nature.

As she gazed at the multitude of dishes, ready to be popped into the oven on Thanksgiving morn, tears pricked Gemma's eyes. "I know what I'll be most thankful for this Thanksgiving." She looked at them. "Friends like you," she rasped.

Maggie hugged her. GeorgeAnne, not a hugger, patted her shoulder.

Kara glanced at her watch. "You can't go yet. Not until—"

A light blue vintage Volkswagen Beetle chugged into the driveway and parked next to Gemma's car.

Kara smiled. "Not until Maddie gets here with the pies. She was running a holiday pie special today. Buy one, get another fifty percent off."

The curly-haired, always effervescent baker launched from her car. "The pies have sold like hot cakes." Eyes twinkling, she retrieved two aluminum-wrapped pie tins from the back seat. "After Kara called in your pie SOS, I saved a pumpkin pie and a pecan pie for you."

Gemma reached for her handbag, but Kara shook her head. "All taken care of. A welcome-to-Truelove gift from the Mason Jar and Madeline's."

She gave Kara and young Maddie a hug. "I can't thank you enough for everything you've done. You've been the true definition of community."

"It's the beginning of my busy season, otherwise I would've been here for the rest of the fun today." Maddie grinned. "But I promise to give you a private pie-making lesson after the holidays."

But the New Year would find Gemma far from Truelove. She swallowed. "That's kind of you, but I'm only in Truelove temporarily. The agency promised to send another care-giver by January."

"That's a shame." GeorgeAnne cleared her throat. "You'll be missed."

She blinked. *Who was this person and what had they done with the real GeorgeAnne Allen?* The older woman's attitude toward her had seemingly done an about-face. She wasn't sure why, but she was grateful.

Gemma swallowed. "I'll miss all of you, too." And she meant it, even the curmudgeonly Truelove matchmaker.

She headed to the ranch. The reminder of her leave-taking left her feeling empty.

It was a disconcerting sensation—to feel such connection to a place and one family in particular. With the exception of Juliet, she'd made a habit of not getting too attached to humans.

She didn't like the idea of needing anyone. Though she'd certainly needed the combined efforts of Truelove's gracious matrons today.

At the farm, Nathan was on the porch. A sudden lump burned her throat.

She hurried out of the car. "Is everything okay with Ike?" There was no sign of Tom Arledge's truck, though he'd prom-ised to sit with Ike until she returned.

"Everything's fine." Nathan leaned against the railing. "The boys and I finished the chores early so I sent Tom home. Dad and the little guys are working on a puzzle."

A sweet relief washed over her. She opened the trunk and retrieved the box of dishes.

He came over to the car. "Let me take that. It looks heavy."

Taking the box, he sniffed the air appreciably. "Something smells delicious. Sounds like you and the ladies were cook-ing up a feast."

She cocked her head. "How—"

"Truelove grapevine." He grinned. "Bridger and the twins

sought refuge at the ranch for lunch. He told me about the hen party at his house." Nathan trudged up the steps. "I hope you had fun. You work too hard."

Flitting ahead, she held the door for him. "Says the hardest-working man I've ever known."

Inside the kitchen, he set the box on the counter. "I think we both need to make a plan for some fun." He took one of the covered casseroles out of the box and handed it to her.

She put the dish in the fridge. "What does it say about us that we have to plan for fun? How boring am I?"

Nathan handed her another container. "You're the least boring person I know. We're superresponsible people with busy lives who have a lot of people and animals depending on us. I admire the work you do, Gemma. How you've helped us." A warmth lit his face.

Her pulse leaped. Hiding her confusion, she put the dish on the refrigerator shelf. When she felt steady enough to face him, she turned around to find he'd lifted the foil on the pecan pie. Caught out, he reddened. She chuckled.

"Maddie Lovett made the pies." She fiddled with the gold hoop at her earlobe. "There wasn't time to make them myself."

He snitched a tiny bit of crust and popped it in his mouth. "Love Maddie's pies, but what I'm looking forward to most is spending Thanksgiving together with you."

Connor and Kody trudged into the kitchen. "We're hungry," Kody declared. "When's supper?"

Nathan shook his head. "Bottomless pits." Ike and Rascal soon followed, also wanting dinner.

"Guys!" He threw out his hands. "Gemma's trying to put together Thanksgiving."

"Which is why tonight's dinner is every man for himself." She pointed to the fridge. "Do me a favor and clean out the leftovers Kara brought from the Jar. I need room for the turkey."

With the guys on microwave duty, she got to work thawing

the turkey per Kara's safe-practice guidelines. Gemma wasn't bothered with so many people in the kitchen. Despite her usually solitary existence, she liked having the boys underfoot, the noise and the commotion they wrought in their wake.

Once she returned to her apartment in Greensboro, she wasn't sure how she'd ever get used to the quiet again. But for now, she intended to soak up every last morsel of joy, like a biscuit sopping gravy. Which, thanks to Kara, she now knew how to make.

Like Nathan, what she was looking forward to the most was spending time with all of them. Especially the man she admired more than any other in the world. Not only for his commitment to care for his ailing father, his devotion to his sons, but also—and she wasn't too proud to admit it—for how he made her feel.

Seventeen again. With the whole world and a lifetime of possibilities yet before her.

Chapter Ten

Thanksgiving Day dawned crisp and cold. Overnight, the temperature had plummeted. Snow was forecast over the holiday weekend.

Filled with anticipation, Gemma awoke early to get a jump start on a timetable that would have rivaled D-Day. She didn't bother putting on fancy clothes. She'd change into something more festive later.

Donning jeans and an old gray sweatshirt, she hurried into the darkened kitchen. Getting the turkey into the oven was her first priority.

She hadn't been in the kitchen fifteen minutes before Nathan joined her. Downing a quick cup of coffee, he scanned her to-do list. Padding into the kitchen, Rascal availed himself of the new doggy exit. The little door flapped behind him.

A blast of frigid air followed in his wake.

"Brrrr..." She reached for her coat hanging on the peg. "I think I left my purse in the car last night."

"I'll get it for you. Stay inside where it's warm. I'm headed outside anyway." Nathan shrugged into his heavy, fleece-lined coat. "I have to chop through the ice so the cattle can drink."

On frosty winter mornings, he was the kind of guy who had probably warmed the car for his wife. A woman would be blessed to have him as her husband. A woman like her?

A ridiculous notion, but she smiled at him. "Thank you. Happy Thanksgiving."

Nathan smiled back. "You're welcome, and happy Thanksgiving to you, too."

Her heart ticked up a notch. *Just because he smiles at you... Stop being such a teenager.*

Nathan put on his work gloves. "I'll be back to help." There was another rush of air as he went outside.

Seconds later, Rascal bounded into the house once more.

Gemma gave him a hug. "Good dog." His fluffy fur was cold against her face. The collie disappeared down the hall to resume his protective watch over Ike.

Wistful for the home she'd always longed for and never known, she took out the odd assortment of items she'd bought on a whim yesterday. She wasn't sure why she'd purchased the ingredients for her mom's corn pudding. Everything else on the menu was a Crenshaw family tradition.

Perhaps she'd merely wanted to bring something of herself— one of the few good things she'd carried from her own dysfunctional childhood.

She'd been angry with her mom for so long—unreasonably so—for failing to fix the toxic atmosphere with Gemma's dad. But most of all, for failing to rescue them until it was far, far too late.

Yet putting together the recipe made her feel close to her mother in a way she hadn't felt since the tragic events of that long-ago day. The ending of her family had been so painful she'd developed the habit of pushing her memories of her mother away. As if her mother had never existed.

But in pushing away the bad, how much of the good had she lost, too?

It made no sense to blame the parent who'd been most wronged for the situation. Yet she had.

Over the months that followed the tragedy, a host of trauma

counselors had cautioned her that until she was ready to find compassion for her mother's all-too-human fragility, and come to terms with the harrowing consequences of her mother's ultimate act of courage, she'd never be free to move forward into her own future.

Frowning, she opened the can of cream-style corn. Why, of all days, was she thinking about this now? But grief never paid a house call when it was convenient. Certainly not when she was in the midst of preparations for Thanksgiving dinner.

On that cold November morning, for the first time in a long time she missed her mom. Really allowed herself to miss her.

It had been her mother who passed on a love for God's creatures. Her mother who taught her to read her Bible and pray. Who encouraged Gemma. Cheered her every endeavor. Who loved her.

Her mother, isolated by her father from friends and relatives, uneducated and with few options for escape, bound to a controlling, abusive narcissist. Finding herself in an impossible situation, her mother had done the best she knew how.

With God's help, wasn't that all anyone could do? Stifling a sob, Gemma put her hand to her mouth.

Standing over the uncooked corn pudding, with the hindsight of maturity, she found compassion in her heart for what her mother had suffered. For everything they'd suffered together.

Then, amid much silent weeping lest she wake the boys or Ike, she forgave her mother the hardest thing of all—for dying. In sacrificing herself, she'd saved Gemma's life. Yet her death had shattered Gemma. Leaving her to face an unknown future alone.

"Gemma?"

Her head shot up. Concern darkening his features, Nathan stood in the doorway. Such had been her grief, she hadn't heard the telltale squeak of the door.

She felt her cheeks burn crimson.

Why did she have to break down now? And in front of Nathan of all people?

Toeing out of his boots, Nate crossed the room. "What's wrong?" He laid her purse on the island stool.

Frantically, she swiped at the tears coursing across her face. "I'm fine."

Nate peeled off his gloves and stuffed them in his coat pockets. "You're not fine. What's happened to make you feel sad?"

"Holidays bring reminders of people no longer in my life." Taking a shaky breath, she fluttered her hand as if waving her cares away. "Sorry for being such a downer. I should dice the apples for the dressing."

She tried to move past him, but he stopped her with a gentle touch on her arm. "Believe me, Gemma, I understand all too well."

Her stomach twisted. "You lost your wife. Of course you understand." She dropped her eyes to the floor. "Forgive me for being insensitive."

Capturing her chin between his thumb and index finger, he lifted her gaze to meet his. "Gemma."

Tears like tiny dewdrops clung to the edges of her lashes. Tenderness filled him.

"Dad is fond of saying that pain shared is pain halved. Talk to me." The knot in his belly tightened. "Tell me what you're thinking and feeling."

Her chin quivered. "You should take your own advice."

Nate dropped his hand. "I… I can't." He tugged at the back of his neck. "I'm sorry."

Surprisingly, it was Gemma who comforted him. She squeezed his hand. "It's taken me a long time to battle through the baggage to the feelings I experienced this morning."

"Which are...?" He shook his head. "Sorry. I've no right to probe."

"Ike is right. It is better to share it with someone." She sighed. "Making her corn pudding, I found myself missing my mom. How's that for crazy?"

"Not crazy." He prayed she wouldn't shut him down. "You never talked about your family. Is your mother still living?"

Gemma stared out the window at the swaths of pink and gold in the sky over the mountains. "Sadly, no."

Shoulder to shoulder with her, he kept his gaze trained on the rolling pastureland beyond the window. Sometimes confidences were easier shared without eye contact.

Gemma sighed. "My mother died the day I got home from camp."

His eyes jerked to hers. He scanned her face. Not what he'd expected. But maybe that explained something about what happened between him and Gemma.

She let go of his hand to tuck a tendril of hair behind her ear. Immediately, he missed the warmth of her hand in his.

Burnt orange, her ribbon of the day, reminded him of autumn leaves on the nearby Blue Ridge Parkway.

"I'm sorry." Finding her hand again, he laced his fingers through hers. She didn't pull away. "You must've been devastated."

"You would think so, wouldn't you?" She gave a self-deprecating laugh devoid of mirth. "But anger is easier than devastation."

"I get it."

Her eyes darted to him.

"As shields go, there's nothing better than anger to keep from feeling the pain." Or in his case, the guilt. "Anything to keep at bay the grief."

She tilted her head. "You don't seem angry to me."

He hunched his shoulders. "Anger is the fuel driving my

workaholism. Which you were right to call me on. I'm trying to change. To do better for the boys and Dad."

"I see how hard you try." Her mouth wobbled. "Your efforts do not go unappreciated by your family. Or me," she whispered.

Bringing her hand to his mouth, he brushed his lips across her fingers. "I'm sorry Thanksgiving recalled tough memories."

Her eyes glistened with tears.

For the past two weeks, it had taken everything in him not to gather her into his arms. The desire to cradle her, to hold her in the circle of his arms, intensified. He fought himself no more.

Nate put his arms around her. He kept his hold loose, letting her decide to break free or not. But turning into him, she put her face against his shoulder. He buried his nose in her hair.

Over the last few weeks, he hadn't allowed himself to get this close to her. For a moment, she let him hold her. She seemed to find comfort in his embrace. But neither of them were the naive teenagers they'd been.

His chest heaved. "Gem—"

A commotion sounded down the hall.

The boys, his dad and the dog stampeded into the kitchen. Wrenching free, she planted herself next to the island and folded her arms around her sweatshirt.

Placing his palms flat on the edge of the countertop, he leaned over the sink, willing his heartbeat to regulate.

Connor's nose twitched. "Something smells awesome."

"I'm hungry," Kody said.

Slowly, he angled.

Gemma swiped her index finger under her eyes. "You're always hungry."

To his ears, her dry, husky laughter felt a tad hollow. Was she having as hard a time regaining her equilibrium as him?

She handed Kody a cereal bowl. "A light breakfast this morning, if you please, gentlemen. Everyone needs to save their big appetite for all the food I'm cooking."

"We're here to help, right, guys?" He was proud of how even his tone sounded, but his heart continued to drum furiously against his rib cage. "Put us to work."

He might have pulled off normalcy with his sons, but his father gave him a swift, calculating look.

Becoming brisk, she put Nate to work peeling potatoes. When the timer buzzed, he took the turkey out of the oven for her. His dad and the boys were appointed with setting the dining room table.

She'd unearthed harvest decorations, including the large ceramic turkey that had graced every Thanksgiving meal until Deanna died.

While he assembled the deviled eggs, she bustled around, putting the finishing touches on several dishes. His father, the boys and Rascal trouped outside to scavenge for further table decor. They returned with a basket of pine cones and small boughs of cedar. The house filled with the tangy aroma of evergreens and the mouth-watering scent of roasted turkey.

Once the turkey cooled sufficiently to handle, she put him in charge of carving the bird. With organized chaos reigning in the kitchen, he carried the roasting pan and a white platter to the breakfast alcove, where they ate most of their meals.

His dad pulled out the chair next to him. Rascal plopped at his feet. Anointing himself chief taste tester, his father sneaked bits of turkey to Rascal underneath the table.

At the island, she helped the boys roll dough and cut out the biscuits. Kody brandished the rolling pin like a knight of old. Connor and Gemma laughed themselves silly at his silliness.

Flour soon coated most surfaces, but she didn't seem to mind. Smiling, she kissed the dusting of flour on Connor's cheek, which prompted Kody to throw a handful of flour directly into his face. He sputtered. Connor hooted, but Gemma gave Kody a quick peck on his forehead.

His dad chuckled. "She's good with the boys. They really like her."

Nate distrusted the mischievous look in his father's eyes.

Wresting his attention from the hilarity ensuing around him to turkey carving, he concentrated on not slicing off a finger. "It's good they like her since she's helping us over the holidays."

She placed the biscuit tray in the oven and set the timer. "Boys, stand here and watch the biscuits. Make sure they don't get too brown."

Gemma took off her apron. "I'm going to change out of these old work clothes, but if the timer dings before I get back, let your dad take the biscuits out of the oven."

She ambled over to him and his father. "Looks like you have everything under control."

His dad winked at her. "That's because, as the Crenshaw family quality control engineer, I'm keeping a close eye on him." He jerked his thumb in Nate's direction.

Smiling, she disappeared down the hall. Peering through the oven glass, the boys' attention remained riveted on the slowly browning tops of the biscuits.

Leaning closer, his father plucked a morsel of succulent meat off the platter and passed it to Rascal. "The boys aren't the only ones that like her."

Nate raised his eyebrow. "We all like and admire Gemma. She's great."

"My mind may be going, but it isn't gone yet, son. The boys and I interrupted something between you earlier."

"I have no idea what you're talking about, Dad. Gemma and I are just old friends."

His father snorted. "Back in the day, you were head over

heels for that little gal. And from the way you look at her when you think no one's looking, you still are."

"I do not look—" He pressed his lips together.

Ecstatic over getting a rise out of him, his father grinned. "'Course I'm not saying she doesn't look at you the same way, too."

"She does?" Clutching the carving knife, he straightened. "I mean…" Sweat peppered his forehead. "I'm sure you must be mistaken."

His father cackled.

The timer dinged.

"Dad!" Kody shouted.

Saved by the timer.

Ending the awkward conversation with his matchmaking father, he hurried to remove the tray from the oven.

"I heard the—" She dashed into the kitchen. "How are the biscuits?"

The breath knocked from his lungs, his eyes widened. *Wow.*

Kody touched the tip of his finger to the hem of the silky, moss green blouse she wore over her jeans. "You look so pwetty, Miss Gemma, doesn't she, Dad?"

The girl had been pretty. The woman was beautiful. His heart lodged in his throat. Something until now he'd believed an anatomical impossibility.

"Uh…" He opened his mouth. Closed it. Opened it again. "Ummm…"

"What my son is trying and failing miserably to say is, 'Yes, you do.'" Getting out of his chair, his father gave Gemma a hug. "You look a right treat, my dear."

Avoiding eye contact with Nate, she blushed. "Thank you, Mr. Ike. And you, too, Sir Kody." Ducking her head, she exclaimed over his sons' first foray into baking.

The boys were ridiculously proud of the biscuits. Somehow

the food managed to arrive on the table, steaming hot, all at the same time. The credit was entirely hers.

"If you'd allow me?" His dad smiled at each one seated around the dining room table. "I'd like to say grace, son."

"Of course, Dad." He studied his father's bright gaze. "Go ahead."

His dad's prayer was short but heartfelt. He thanked the Lord for the bounty they would partake of, for the hands that prepared it, for the opportunity to be together and for the blessing of loved ones no longer with them. "Amen."

Opening his eyes, Nate cleared his throat. "Amen." Across the table, Gemma drew his gaze like a magnet.

"Amen," she whispered.

They dug in. He relished the happy faces of his sons and his father. Gemma had made this day a wonderful occasion.

It did his heart good to behold his father's returning confidence and quality of life restored. Gemma and Rascal had done that. The future was unknowable, but today—his vision blurred—if only for today, he had his dad back.

Everyone made much of Gemma's corn pudding.

"Good as dessert," his dad proclaimed.

A warm glow softened her features. "I'm glad you like it."

Kody stabbed a slice of turkey with his fork. "This was a gweat idea."

He cut his eyes at his youngest son. "What is, Kode?"

"Thanksgiving."

"Dude…" Connor threw out his hands. "We do Thanksgiving every year."

"Are you sure?" Kody bunched his eyebrows. "I don't 'member anything like this." The little boy's eyes flicked to the ceramic turkey centerpiece. "Butterball looks familiar, though."

Nate's heart constricted.

Deanna had put out the porcelain turkey every Thanksgiving. He'd suspected Kody might not remember much about his mother. He'd only been three when she died so suddenly.

The confirmation of what he'd feared brought him no small measure of pain. Deanna had loved the boys so much. He needed to do better at keeping her memory alive for her sons.

"Oh, no." Scraping back her chair, Gemma jumped up from the table.

His pulse quickened. "What?" He started to rise.

She waved him into his seat. "I forgot to put together the cranberry gelatin salad from the recipe box." Her face fell. "I'm so sorry, guys."

Connor lanced a green bean. "I like the canned stuff better anyway."

"Me, too," Kody chimed.

Nate was reasonably sure Kody had no recollection of cranberry sauce, either way. But whatever his brother liked, Kody liked, too.

"I agree," Nate rasped. "Who needs the gelatin salad? The nuts get stuck in your teeth."

She flashed him a smile. "I see where Kody gets it from."

"Gets what?"

"The endearing silliness." Her brown eyes gleamed. "Thank you."

"It is I who thank you."

A gentle smile lifted the corners of her lips. "For what?"

"For making this the happiest of Thanksgivings for Dad and the boys." His gaze found hers. "And me."

The clink of silverware and the hum of voices momentarily faded. There was only him and her. And the dawning awareness pulsing between them.

At that moment, Kody upset his water glass. Vaulting out of their seats, everyone else grabbed a handful of napkins in a vain attempt to stem the flow of liquid from reaching the floor. For a few minutes, chaos again reigned.

But he wouldn't have it any other way.

To his surprise, he felt content. An emotion so long foreign to him, he barely recognized it. Happy, even. There could be no question of why.

Nate's gaze drifted around the table to the people he loved most in the world.

His father, enjoying life in a way he'd feared forever lost. His sons, blossoming under Gemma's nurturing presence.

As for Gemma? He took a quick intake of breath. He'd loved the girl.

Was he falling in love with the woman?

Chapter Eleven

The guys insisted on doing the Thanksgiving cleanup.

Gemma found herself sitting on the sofa in the living room with her feet propped, unsure what to do with such unaccustomed leisure.

From the kitchen came the sound of running water, the clink of silverware deposited in the drawer and the low murmur of conversation. She smiled at the boys' bright chatter.

A few minutes later, Kody ventured into the living room. His feet dragged. He was tired. It had been a full day. He sank onto the couch next to her.

He nestled against her. "Can I tell you a secret, Miss Gemma?"

She tilted her head to get a better look at him. "Of course, sweetie. What is it?"

He sighed. "I don't 'member my mama. Her picture is on my dresser and sometimes I think I see her like when she worked in the garden, but I'm not sure if I'm 'membering, or if it's 'cause Connor told me she liked flowers."

Gemma put her arm around him.

Rubbing his eyes, he laid his head against her shoulder. "Connor says it makes Daddy sad to talk about her so we don't. But I wish I 'membered her."

Gemma's heart pinched.

He yawned. "I'm the only one in my class without a mom. Know what else, Miss Gemma?"

She hugged him closer. "What, sweetie pie?"

"I love you."

A lump settled in her throat. "I love you, too, Kody," she rasped.

His eyelids had closed. Fighting tears, she kissed the top of his hair.

Connor hovered on the other side of the coffee table. "Miss Gemma?"

"Yes, honey?"

He bit his lip. "Is there room on the couch for me?" The yearning on his face just about broke her heart.

She patted the spot on her left. "There's always room for you, Connor."

With a grateful smile, he plopped down beside her. Kody didn't stir. She put her other arm around Connor. They talked for a few minutes about nothing and everything until his eyelids drooped, too.

Blame it on the early morning, the excitement and the tryptophan, but soon both of Nathan's sons were out for the count.

Effectively trapped, she made no move to disturb them. There was no place she'd rather be than with the two dearest little boys in the whole world.

Closing her eyes, she thanked God for her job and dogs like Rascal at PawPals that gave her life purpose. She thanked God for the people He had placed in her life. Juliet and her family. At her lowest point, God had brought the Spencers into her life to give her back her life.

Had God brought her into Kody's and Connor's lives, for even this short time, to do the same?

Overcome with fatigue from a day well spent, she floated in and out of wakefulness.

What was she looking forward to the future?

Her last coherent thought was to wonder if her future would include Nathan.

* * *

His dad had insisted on washing the dishes. Nate dried, and the boys put the dishes away. Eventually, he sent the boys off to play, but they headed into the living room to see what Gemma was doing.

He winced. "Not what I meant when I told them to go have fun."

"Can't say I blame them." His father grinned. "Gemma's a lot of fun."

His dad plucked the leash hanging from the peg on the wall. Tail wagging, Rascal rose to his feet. "Think I'll take a stroll to clear the cobwebs from my head."

Nate went in search of his sons. Stepping into the living room, what he found wasn't what he expected. Both boys were asleep, snuggled against Gemma, who was also asleep. The sweet picture stole his breath.

Despite his initial misgivings, she had proved herself unlike the girl who'd callously broken his heart. This Gemma, the one he was gradually getting to know, was kind and generous. Good with dogs, little boys and ailing old men. Quick to laugh.

But it was hard to reconcile the two Gemmas. Which one was real? Was this Gemma too good to be true just like the teenage Gemma had been?

If his family hadn't walked in on them this morning, would he have kissed her? Part of him had wanted to, but would that have been wise? Doubts warred with the feelings she reawakened inside him.

For his father's sake, he'd opened his home to her. But did he dare open his heart to her? There was so much more at stake. Namely, the hearts of his sons, more precious to him than anything in the world.

They trusted her. Why couldn't he? But the burned child dreads the fire, and he'd already been burned by her once before.

He made a move to backtrack lest he awaken them, but a floorboard squeaked under his foot. Her eyes flew open. The look on her face stopped him cold.

Alarm flared in her expression. As recognition dawned, her gaze cleared. Who or what had taught her to be so hypervigilant?

Her mother died the day she returned from camp. Why wouldn't she tell him what else happened that caused her to end things between him? Why must she be so secretive?

Nate's conscience smote him. *Why can't you talk to her about Deanna?*

"I didn't mean to startle you," he whispered.

The boys didn't stir.

Carefully extricating herself, she placed a cushion under Kody's head and propped Connor against the armrest. Inching to the edge of the sofa, she eased upright.

They tiptoed into the kitchen. She brushed her hair out of her face. "Tell me I wasn't drooling."

"Far from it." His voice gruff, he cleared his throat. "More like Sleeping Beauty."

Her gaze flitted to his and away. "Where's Ike?"

"Gone for his afternoon walk." Leaning against the counter, he crossed his arms over his chest. At his movement, her eyes flickered. "Thank you again for the day you gave my dad and the boys."

A smile softened her lips. "It's me who should thank you for allowing me to share the day with your family."

Her gaze swept over him. His heartbeat stuttered. Swinging around, she opened the refrigerator door. "Are leftovers for dinner okay with you?"

Nate's ribs ached as if he'd run a long, painful distance. "Leftovers are one of the best parts about Thanksgiving." He strived to keep his voice matter-of-fact. "But I hired you to look after Dad, not cook and clean up after us, Gemma."

"I don't mind." She toyed with the end of her braid. "I like looking after you. You and the boys."

He liked the way she looked after him—and the boys—but he mustn't tell her that.

She tucked a strand of hair behind her ear, playing havoc with his nerve endings. "Ike is doing well today. I was concerned he might not be."

He jammed his hands in his jeans. "Why's that?"

"It's usually when patients get overtired that the mental confusion sets in."

He fingered his chin. "Dad seems more like himself than he has been in a long time. I've been trying to take my cues from him. Was that wrong?"

She shook her head. "Allowing him to set the pace within reasonable limits should be fine. We just need to be aware the holidays will tax his mental and physical energy."

Nate sighed. "I can't help wondering if this year will be the last real Christmas he's able to enjoy with us. I want it to be everything he wishes it to be."

She wrapped her hand around his arm. "We'll make sure it's the best Christmas ever for Ike and the boys."

It was amazing how less alone he felt since she returned to his life. A shared burden was truly a halved burden.

The back door squeaked open. His father and Rascal ambled into the kitchen. His dad's cheeks were rosy from the cold, and his eyes shone. His father had always loved the outdoors. Being confined to the house so much was a trial for him. But thanks to Rascal, his dad could still enjoy a measure of independence.

His father eased into a chair. "Where's the boys?" Rascal plopped onto the floor beside his feet.

"They're taking a nap." He grinned. "Thanksgiving wore them out."

"Me, too." His father laughed. "But before I get a little shut-eye, I wanted to make sure we're going to set up the Christmas tree tomorrow as usual."

Nate exchanged a look with Gemma. "If you aren't too tired."

His dad waved his hand. "It's a Crenshaw family tradition to decorate the tree the day after Thanksgiving. The boys will be disappointed if we don't."

"Let's see how you're feeling tomorrow morning, but if you're still gung ho, we'll head out to the Christmas tree farm."

His father smiled. "Great."

Nate hoped his dad would still be as clear-eyed tomorrow. The boys would be disappointed if the annual Christmas tree expedition didn't happen.

These days, one day at a time was the most Nate could manage. Who was he kidding? What was the use in dreaming?

Anything—much less love—beyond his father's illness felt totally out of reach.

That night, Nathan warned the boys the Christmas tree hunt would be dependent upon how their grandfather felt the next day.

Friday morning was another beautiful blue-sky, cold winter day. At breakfast, Gemma could see the boys struggling to contain their excitement. They'd rushed out first thing to tend to the animals. But all through toast and oatmeal, they were on tenterhooks waiting for Ike to appear.

Please, God... She sent a quick prayer skyward. *Let Ike have another good day for the boys' sake.* She glanced at their father, His posture stiff, he stirred brown sugar into his oatmeal. *For Nathan's, too.*

Rascal was first into the kitchen. Shoulders bowed, Ike trod heavily behind him. Her heart sank. Not a good sign.

Spoons halfway to their mouths, the boys froze. Hope

dimmed in their faces. Nathan's eyes flickered. A line furrowed his brow.

Broadening his chest, Ike grinned. "Anyone up for Christmas tree hunting this morning?"

Eyebrows arched like a question mark, the boys' gazes cut to Nathan. She held her breath.

Nathan put down his spoon. "Since the morning chores are done, I think something could be arranged." He smiled.

"Yahoo!" Kody fist-pumped the air.

She released the breath she'd been holding. Connor didn't say anything, but happiness shone from his face. Catching the general air of excitement, Rascal gave a quick, short bark.

Ike ran his hand across the collie's fur. "A banner day for us all."

After breakfast, the boys made a mad scramble to find their coats, hats and mittens. She donned her puffy black overcoat and wound a woolen teal scarf around her neck. She tucked her hair into the matching teal knit hat atop her head. Then they were off.

Rascal sat secured between the boys in the rear of the crew cab. With Ike riding shotgun, she took the middle front seat in Nathan's slate gray, six-seater, full-size truck.

"Sorry for the tight fit," he apologized. "The tree farm isn't far. On the other side of the ridge."

Buckling her seat belt, she faced forward. "I'm fine."

At the sign for the Morgan Tree Farm, he veered off the rural road onto a long, graveled driveway. Between standing rows of evergreens, she caught her first glimpse of the Morgan family homestead.

The tin-roofed, two-story white farmhouse with a wraparound porch and a stone chimney crowned the top of a knoll. Behind the house lay a barn and a white outbuilding. Acres of Christmas trees surrounded the entire complex. In the distance, the smoky purple Blue Ridge Mountains undulated like the folds of a fan.

Ike gestured toward the horizon. "Purty parcel of land, isn't it?"

She sniffed. "Nothing beats cattle grazing on the gently rolling hills of the High Country Ranch, though."

Ike grinned. "A woman with impeccable taste. Surest way to a rancher's heart."

She tilted her head. "What's that?"

"Love me, love my steers." Mischief gleamed from his gaze. "Or at least my son's heart, right, Nate my boy?"

Nathan rolled his eyes.

She chuckled. "For a K-9 trainer, it's love me, love my dog."

"I hope you made a note of that, son. The way to this woman's heart is through a dog."

He shot his father a look. "Dad..."

She nudged his shoulder. "Your father is an incurable romantic."

Nathan shook his head. "He's something, all right."

Following the driveway behind the house, he parked between the barn and the farm store. The parking lot was already three-quarters full. The boys and Ike got out of the truck. Ike unbuckled Rascal, but kept him on a leash. Nathan came around to assist her out of the pickup.

His hand felt warm and strong against her skin. "Thank you." The calluses on his palm bore testimony to his hard work.

For a second, his gaze locked with hers. His eyes went a darker shade of blue. Her stomach somersaulted.

His father coughed gently. "Looks like the Morgan Open House is off to a promising start."

Nathan broke eye contact first.

Pulling on her gloves, she took a deep breath of the tangy,

evergreen-scented air. Garlands and wreaths hung on the lattice surrounding the broad porch of the white outbuilding.

A pleasant-faced man a few years younger than her and Nathan came forward with a firm grasp on a blond, towheaded little boy about three years old. "I wasn't sure we'd see you this year, Mr. Ike."

Ike beamed. "Gemma, meet Luke Morgan, our favorite Christmas tree farmer."

"Better known as Jeremiah's dad." The pride in his voice was evident. Luke placed his palm on the little boy's hooded coat. "Nice to meet you, ma'am."

She smiled at the little boy with the big blue eyes.

Kody wiggled his fingers. "Hey, Jeremiah."

Ducking his head, the child smiled.

Ike patted his canine companion. "This here gorgeous creature is my new buddy, Rascal."

Hearing his name, the dog woofed.

Ike planted his hands on his hips. "We're on a mission to find the most perfect Christmas tree ever, isn't that right, boys?"

Luke batted the furry pom attached to Connor's orange-striped knit cap. "You've come to the right place then. Go see my sister, Krista." He motioned toward a young woman with long, curly brown hair handing handsaws to customers. "She'll get you started."

The boys surged forward. Ike and Rascal, too.

"Hang there a minute," Nathan called. "I'll be the one in charge of the saw."

"Guys? Wait for me." As he raced after Nathan's boys, Jeremiah's small legs churned. "This year, I give out de carts."

"That's right, son." Luke winked at Nathan. "Get to work."

"Dibs on the cart," Connor shouted.

"But Dad…" Kody wailed.

"You'll take turns hauling it up the mountain." Nathan

flicked an amused glance at Luke. "Got your boy on the payroll already?"

He laughed. "You know how it is with family-owned operations. Put 'em to work young and train 'em right."

Nathan looked around. "Where's your better half?"

"Shayla's manning the storefront. She'll ring up your ticket while I put the tree through the baler. Be sure and introduce Gemma to my sisters and my wife."

Nathan nudged her. "You'll probably recognize Shayla Morgan from television."

"*The* Shayla Morgan?" She gaped at the young Christmas tree farmer. "The country music star whose 'Cradle Lullaby' tops the charts every Christmas is your wife?"

"Hard to believe, isn't it?"

She blushed to the soles of her boots. "I didn't mean—"

"Every time I look at her, I wonder the same." He chuckled. "How I ever came to be blessed with someone as wonderful as her in my life."

She smiled. "I've been a fan since her first recording hit the airwaves."

He clapped a hand to Nathan's back. "Your dad is looking more like his old self."

Nathan rubbed his jaw. "It's amazing what an assistance dog and Gemma can do in two weeks."

At his praise, her cheeks went crimson. "I'm thankful Ike is back to living his best possible life."

"Dad! Miss Gemma!" Returning, Connor and Kody tugged at their arms.

"Quit your jawin' and get over here!" Ike yelled. "Us lumberjacks got Christmas trees to fell."

Nathan took possession of the handsaw. Connor pulled the cart up the incline. Ike and Rascal took point on the tree-hunting expedition.

At the uphill exertion, she puffed, her breath fogging in

the cold mountain air. "Didn't realize I was so out of shape," she wheezed.

"Such a flatlander," Nathan teased. "Thin mountain air. You'll get used to it."

For a split second, the idea of searching for the perfect Christmas tree every year over multiple Christmas futures flashed across her vision.

She sneaked a glance in Nathan's direction. A lovely dream, but of course not her future. Good things like that didn't happen to her.

"Miss Gemma!" Kody shrieked. It was his turn at pulling the cart. "Come see the one I found!"

Sucking in a lungful of oxygen, she plunged onward.

Reaching a largely untouched section midway on the hill, the boys dashed about, proclaiming the merits of this tree and that one. Eventually, two top contenders emerged. Ike cast the deciding vote for a perfectly proportioned six-foot Fraser fir.

She removed the red price tag and handed it to Kody for safekeeping. Crouching at the base, Nathan placed the saw against the trunk and commenced cutting.

"Timber!" Kody hollered.

Keeping one hand on Rascal's leash and the other on the tree to keep it from toppling over, Ike chortled. With the cut tree placed atop the cart, they descended to the farm store. More people had arrived. Everyone called out greetings.

It gave her a warm, fuzzy feeling to realize how many people stopped to welcome her, too. She had lived in Greensboro most of her adult life. Yet she didn't know as many people there as she'd met after only two weeks in friendly little Truelove.

Ike chatted up a storm with two of his ROMEO compadres. Rascal sat on his haunches, his brown-eyed gaze fixed in rapt attention on Ike's animated face. The boys played hide-and-seek with a passel of children behind various Christmas trees up and down the hilly terrain.

Her gaze drifted to Nathan, talking to tall, lanky Clay. As if drawn, his eyes lifted to hers and held. A blush rose in her cheeks that had less to do with the frosty morning and more to do with the bond connecting them since one long-ago, unforgettable summer.

Burying her face in the steam rising from her cup, she ventured to the far end of the porch. Nathan joined her. As always, her pulse did a quick staccato whenever she found herself close to him.

"I didn't realize the extent of the Morgan Open House." She pressed her lips against the rim of the cup.

"You can count on Truelove to make any event, large or small, an occasion." Surveying the tree-studded hillside, he gripped the porch railing. "Any excuse to get folks together."

She warmed her hands around the cup. "I like how the town supports one another."

His eyes cut to her and slid away. "What we lack in size, we make up with heart."

And then some. Her heart clanged like sleigh bells against her rib cage.

But abruptly, without warning, he turned away.

Chapter Twelve

Feeling the sudden chill between them, Gemma knotted her hands. Perhaps it was only her who harbored these ridiculous feelings from the past.

Nathan motioned toward the bedecked wreaths and garlands. "We should probably get a few decorations for the house."

After picking out two wreaths and a swath of garland for the mantel, she followed him inside the small farm shop to pay for their purchases. She finally met the talented and very sweet Shayla Morgan.

For Gemma, it was a total fan-girl moment, much to Nathan's apparent amusement. Whatever had prompted him to turn away from her appeared to have passed.

With the tree strapped into the bed of the truck, they headed home, singing Christmas carols at the top of their lungs. The rest of the day, they decorated the tree and the farmhouse with ornaments from the boxes Nathan and Ike hauled out of the attic.

That night, long after everyone had gone to bed, she sat in the living room. Except for the glow of the multicolored lights on the Christmas tree, the room was dark.

A lump rose in her throat. It truly was the most perfect tree ever.

The back door creaked. Seconds later, Nathan's broad shoulders filled the doorframe. "Oh, hi."

"Hey." She unfolded from the couch. "I didn't realize any-one was still awake."

"I needed to check on a heifer." He shuffled his stocking feet. "I saw the tree shining through the window and figured Dad must've left on the lights."

She sighed. "I wasn't ready for the day to end."

"It was a fun day." He moved toward the tree. "You're such a good sport about everything Dad and the boys throw at you."

She'd believed Thanksgiving to be the best day ever, but each day spent with Nathan and his family felt better than the last.

"Thank you for staying on through the holidays until we can get a permanent caregiver for Dad."

"You don't have to keep thanking me." The last thing she wanted was his gratitude. "It's been my pleasure entirely."

"Still, we've taken you away from your usual celebrations with family and friends."

"No family." She crossed her arms over her sweater. "I don't do much in the way of decorating my apartment in Greens-boro. Seems a lot of trouble with only me to enjoy it."

He frowned. "You don't spend Christmas alone, do you?"

Not meeting his gaze, she shrugged. "I attend a Christmas Eve service with Juliet's family and her mom. Then Rob's aunt and uncle host a small party at their farmhouse. After that, I drive back from Laurel Grove to my apartment."

He stared at her. "But what about Christmas morning?"

She blew out a breath. "Christmas morning is best enjoyed by families unwrapping their gifts without the unnecessary burden to entertain an outsider like me."

"The last two days—the last two weeks—wouldn't have been the same without you." His brow creased. "I hope you don't feel like an outsider with us."

"Actually, I don't."

Not even once. The feeling of belonging was something she hadn't experienced in a long time.

He glanced at something outside the window. "Would you look at that?"

Illuminated by the floodlight on the corner of the house, tiny snowflakes drifted lazily from the darkened night sky.

She rushed to the window for a better look. "Ohhh…"

"The first snowfall." He caught her hand. "Let's go out and enjoy it."

"But it's late."

He cocked his head. "Not too late, I hope."

Was he referring to more than the time of day? Her pulse quickened. Something sweet swelled in her heart. "It's never too late."

He grinned. "Come on then. Grab your coat, and let's get out there."

In the kitchen, she retrieved her coat, scarf and gloves. She stepped into the ankle boots she'd left by the door. He clapped his Stetson onto his head and donned his boots again.

He drew her into the yard. The snow was coming down heavier, covering the ground. Feeling like a kid, she lifted her face to the sky and closed her eyes.

Arms outstretched, she did a slow three-sixty. The snowflakes skimmed her cheeks with the delicate grace of a butterfly. "Should we wake the boys?"

"Let's not," he rasped.

She opened her eyes. Something unreadable flickered across his features.

"They'll get their fill of snow in the morning." Taking off a glove, he caught the edge of a snowflake, trembling on the end of her eyelashes, with the tip of his forefinger.

"Let this first snowfall be for us." His Adam's apple bobbed in his throat. "You and me." His gaze moved to her mouth.

Her knees melted. Was he going to kiss her? Did she want him to kiss her? Her heart pounded.

"Would it be okay if I kissed you?" He gulped. "I've been wanting to since the day you arrived."

Reason warred against the feelings churning in her gut. This was a bad idea. She was leaving in a month. Why was she even thinking about—

"Yes," she whispered.

His breath felt warm against her cheek. He tilted his head. Her lips parted. He brushed his mouth against hers.

Gemma's innate, well-earned caution blared warnings of danger ahead, but for once she didn't listen.

The press of his lips was the tenderest of touches. Something she'd believed would never happen again with him, her first and only love.

It had been so long since she'd felt happiness of any sort. So what if she was only here another four weeks? Why not seize any happiness by the fistful while she could? Soon enough, she'd return to her usual solitude.

She didn't delude herself anything long-term could ever come from this most unexpected reunion. Too much had happened. Their lives were on different trajectories, but if their paths intersected only for Christmas…why not?

A blast of sudden cold air jolted her back to reality. Nathan had taken a step away. She shivered.

"Gemma?" His voice deepened. "It was okay I kissed you, wasn't it?"

It was better than okay. It was simply everything. The snow continued to fall around them.

He raked his hand over his head. "I shouldn't have kissed you."

And though she'd been thinking the same, it hurt to hear him speak her thoughts aloud.

"There's so much upheaval in my life right now. I'm not in a position to pursue a relationship with anyone."

Gemma took a quick, indrawn breath. "Of course. I understand."

"Sometimes the loneliness gets to me."

"Me, too," she rasped.

"Once upon a time, you and me somehow seemed so..."

She swallowed past the boulder in her throat. "Right?"

He shook his head. "I was thinking *inevitable*, but *unfinished* works, too. Yet now..."

Closure, Ike had called it.

"You don't have to explain, Nathan."

He blew out a breath. "I've been stuck in limbo since Deanna died."

The stark anguish in his eyes pierced Gemma to the core.

"I've been frozen. But with you, I feel..." He threw out his hands. "I don't rightly know how I feel. But it scares the stuffing out of me."

"You mean the dressing?"

A ghost of a smile quirked his mouth. "The last thing I want to do is hurt you, Gemma. Nor get hurt, either."

She wasn't the naive teenage girl he'd once courted. She was a strong woman. A woman who knew how to protect her heart.

"Nobody dreads getting hurt more than me, but here's what I learned over fifteen painful years. Life is risky."

"I can't make you any promises, Gemma."

"Right back at you." She held up her hands, palms raised. "No expectations here."

He pursed his lips. "We don't want to make a spectacle of ourselves and give the Truelove grapevine more grist for the gossip mill."

She nodded. "Let's just enjoy Christmas."

If in the process, they helped each other heal, to get past their individual roadblocks, so much the better.

She might be helping Nathan move on toward the next love in his life. But the boys needed a mother. He deserved to find love again. Even if it wasn't with her.

What did she want?

To be happy.

If only for this briefest of seasons.

Nate lay awake half the night pondering every possible disastrous ramification of kissing Gemma. What had he been thinking? It wasn't often—as in never—he threw caution to the wind and just reacted.

Lying on his back staring at the darkened ceiling, he felt a wave of terror engulf him. As if he stood on the brink of a precipice of no return. Beneath his proverbial feet, there lay only a bottomless gorge of fear.

This would not—could not—end well. For either of them.

Ever since she returned to his life, there'd been an intense attraction between them. In the wee hours of the night, he rationalized, maybe it was better to get it out in the open.

First loves were powerful, yet probably only in extremely rare cases were they forever loves. He consoled himself he'd been clear about the likelihood of any future relationship. Boundaries ensured their friendship would survive any brief holiday romance.

"No expectations. No promises," he whispered.

Settling the issue in his mind, he finally drifted off to sleep.

The next day, a cold, brittle sunshine beamed from a blue sky. Snow had transformed the ranch into a winter wonderland. The boys were beyond ecstatic at the prospect of a day spent romping in the snow.

After last night, he felt self-conscious with Gemma. He

dragged the sleds out of the barn, and she joined the boys on their downhill runs. His dad and Rascal took a turn, too.

Later that morning, Nate waved them over. "Time to head inside."

"Awww, Dad…" Kody groaned.

Her cheeks bright red from the cold, Gemma had her arm around Connor's shoulder. "You've been out here so long your clothes are wet through."

Kody glowered. "I want to play outside some more."

She tapped the end of Kody's nose with her finger. "Rascal's been out here a long time. His paws are probably freezing."

Connor perked. "Rascal needs snow booties for Christmas."

"I have a gweat idea, guys." Kody bounced up and down. "When we see Santa this afternoon, we could give him Rascal's Christmas wish list."

She cocked her head. "Santa's coming this afternoon?"

"We go see him."

Her gaze pinged between the boys. "You two are heading to the North Pole today?"

Kody giggled.

Smiling, Connor shook his head. "Saturday after Thanksgiving is the Truelove Christmas Parade. We always visit Santa on the Square, don't we, Dad?" His face fell. "Unless Grandpa doesn't feel like going—"

"We always go see Santa. Daddy!" Kody wailed. "Please, please, please…"

He frowned at his son. "Kody, that's enough."

Gemma put her hand on Kody's shoulder. "I'll stay with Ike, Nathan. You take the boys to the—"

"While I appreciate the offer, Gemma—" his father drew himself up "—I can answer for myself, thank you very much."

Nate crossed his arms over his coat. "It's been a busy couple of days. There's no shame in skipping the festival this year, Dad. I wouldn't mind a quiet afternoon at home."

"You stay home and rest then." His father scowled. "I'm not tired."

"There's no point in overdoing things." Nate widened his stance in the snow. "We've had fun over Thanksgiving, but—"

"Don't talk to me like I'm a child," his dad snapped.

"Stop being stubborn," Nate grunted. "I'm trying to look out for you."

"I can look out for myself." His father's voice rose.

"That's just it, Dad." He jabbed his finger in the air between them. "It breaks my heart, but the truth is you can't."

His father became livid. "There's nothing wrong with me that warm clothes and a good, hot lunch won't cure."

"Nathan, please. Ike." Gemma inserted herself between them. "You're scaring the boys."

Connor had gone quiet, too quiet. Kody looked to be on the verge of tears. His sons huddled against Gemma.

Deanna would have known how to defuse the situation before it ever escalated to a shouting match.

Nate slumped. "Fine. Dry clothes. Lunch."

"I won't allow myself to get overtired, I promise." The defiance faded from his dad's gaze. "I'm sorry, son. I hate I've become such a burden to everyone I love."

Nate hugged his father. "You're not a burden, Dad."

His father tugged at Rascal's leash. "I think I'll head in now." His dad and the collie shuffled toward the house.

Ashamed of the example he'd set, Nate crouched beside his sons. "I'm sorry for raising my voice to Granddad. And to you, too."

Kody's lips trembled. "Does this mean we're going to the parade?"

He pinched the bridge of his nose. "I guess so."

"But before y'all go, I think some quiet time for everyone sounds like a great idea." She patted Kody's knit cap. "How about you and Connor set the table for lunch?"

The boys took off at a run, but with a troubled look, Connor spun around. "Miss Gemma, you're coming with us, aren't you?"

She fingered the fringe on the end of her scarf. "Maybe it would be better if I stayed at the ranch."

"Nooo…" Connor protested. "It won't be as much fun without you."

"He's right." Nate cleared his throat. "It won't be as much fun without you."

She looked at him. "Okay, I'll come."

The usually reticent Connor whooped with joy and took off after his little brother.

"Are you okay?" she asked Nate.

"I forgot how quickly Dad can flare up." He shook his head. "I should've handled it better." They headed across the yard toward the house.

"Traveling this journey alongside a loved one with dementia isn't easy." She linked her arm through the crook of his elbow. "It's not you he's really lashing out at. It's the increasing restrictions on his independence that he resents."

Nate heaved a sigh. "It sure feels like it's me he's angry at."

She hugged his arm. "For that, I'm sorry."

At the foot of the porch, he paused. "If you're tired or need a break from us—" He grimaced. "I could use a break from us sometimes—please don't feel you have to go this afternoon."

She fluttered her lashes at him. "Spending the afternoon with Santa, your father, the boys…and you?"

He heard the smile in her voice.

Taking his hands in hers, she rose onto the tips of her toes. "There's no place I'd rather be." She kissed his cheek.

The warmth of her lips tingled against his skin. He felt the same. There was no one he'd rather spend the afternoon with than her.

* * *

Since her last visit, Gemma was amazed at the holiday transformation the little town had undergone. The Parks and Rec Department had been busy.

Heading toward the square with Rascal leashed at his side, Ike elbowed her. "Wait till you get a gander at the matchmaking trio."

"Oh?"

"They double as elves for the Santa on the Square event." He grinned. "Pointed shoes. Floppy hat. Striped stockings. The works."

Nathan laughed. "Boggles the mind, doesn't it?"

Ike grunted. "Worth the trip to Truelove."

From the loudspeakers mounted at the edges of the square, strains of "Winter Wonderland" provided a festive note. Friends called out greetings to the Crenshaws. Greetings to her as well. It looked as if the entire population had turned out for the annual Christmas parade. And for the free hot chocolate, courtesy of the Mason Jar.

In the middle of the green, Santa—aka the mayor—sat enthroned in the gazebo. Next to the mayor, the diminutive Miss IdaLee, oldest of the matchmaking trio, sat on a chair playing Mrs. Santa.

Gemma snapped a photo of Connor on Santa's lap first. In their pint-sized Stetsons and boots, both boys were adorable.

Connor asked for various calf-showing accoutrements for next year's 4-H competition at the county fair. Easing Connor off his lap, Santa steered him toward the grandmotherly ErmaJean on the steps of the gazebo. Her silvery hair tucked into a green felt hat, she resembled a jolly, if somewhat plump, elf. She handed Connor a green-striped candy cane.

As befitted her take-charge demeanor, GeorgeAnne, armed with a clipboard and a whistle, supervised the line of children waiting to talk with Santa. Also in elf attire, she looked more Christmas scarecrow than Santa's helper.

The jolly, Santa look-alike mayor patted Kody's knee. "Have you been a good boy this year?"

An interesting look came over Kody's face. "Well, it's like this, sir." He opened his hands. "I think I've been as good as could be weasonably expected."

Ike chortled. "Lot of personality in that grandson of mine."

Nathan rolled his eyes. "Ain't that the truth."

Gemma hid her smile in her hand.

Santa's blue eyes twinkled. "Tell Santa, young Crenshaw, what you'd like for Christmas?"

"I've given it some thought," the littlest cowboy mused. "I've decided what I want most for Christmas is for Gemma to be my new mommy."

She gasped. GeorgeAnne's eyes behind the frames of her glasses went owllike. IdaLee put her hand to her mouth. "Oh, my."

Oh, my indeed.

"Uhhh, well then…" Santa scratched his neck under the fluffy white collar. "Perhaps your father should field this one?"

Field it he did. Nathan pulled Kody off Santa's lap. His hand clamped onto his son's shoulder. "We're going home."

Kody jutted his jaw. "Santa asked me what I wanted so I told him."

"That is a matter for grown-ups to decide. Not you."

Hands on his hips, Kody glared at his dad. "What's so bad about wanting Gemma to stay with us forever? Connor wants a new mommy, too."

Palms raised, Connor backed away, wanting no part of guilt by association.

The look on Nathan's face… If he hadn't been so mortified, it would have almost been comical.

He towed his son down the gazebo steps. "I don't know what's gotten into you."

"I didn't get a candy cane…" Kody wailed.

"Maybe you should've thought of that before you totally embarrassed Gemma—all of us—in front of everyone." Nathan raked a hand over his head.

His hat fell off. GeorgeAnne picked it up.

Nathan shook his finger at his son. "You and I are going to have a serious talk when we get back to the ranch, about what is and is not appropriate behavior."

GeorgeAnne handed Nathan his hat. "Don't be too hard on him. He was simply expressing his feelings." Her gaze swung to Gemma and back. "Something we should all aspire to do."

ErmaJean thrust a candy cane at Gemma. "For later," she whispered.

The ride to the ranch was accomplished in near silence. Gemma wanted to hug Kody so badly, it hurt like a physical pain.

But squished in the front seat between Ike and Kody's dad, she stared straight ahead through the windshield as the truck ate up the miles between Truelove and the farm.

A day that had begun with such promise… If she'd ever doubted where she stood with him or how he envisioned his future—a future that did not include her—she doubted no more.

He fired a glance in the rearview mirror at his youngest son. "You will go to your room as soon as we get home."

At the house, Ike climbed wearily from the pickup. "Connor, I think Rascal would enjoy meeting the rabbits." They set off. Tears streaking across his face, Kody headed inside.

Nathan stopped her. "Could we talk first?" He sucked in a breath. "I had no idea Kody would say something like that. I'm so sorry."

After the initial shock had worn off, strangely she wasn't.

Kody had been honest. Expressing the deepest desire of his heart. And as she was slowly coming to realize, hers, too.

None of that mattered, of course, since Nathan didn't feel the same.

"Please go easy on him." She bit her lip. "He gave you a glimpse of his heart. That kind of bravery is a rare and beautiful gift."

"But—"

She fluttered her hand. "Forget the particulars of me and you. See what he said for what it truly is—a little boy who doesn't have even a memory of a mother. And it's Christmas."

Nathan sagged against the porch railing. "At the diner the other day after you left, Aunt Georgie told me much the same thing." His gaze slid away. "Among other things."

From his expression, she guessed whatever his great-aunt had said about her had probably not been flattering. But the only thing that mattered was helping Nathan see this moment for what it was—an opportunity for healing.

"If you shut Kody down, he may never open up to you again." She lifted her chin. "Trust me when I tell you, that's not the sort of relationship you want with your son."

He studied her. "You're speaking from experience?"

"I am."

"With the father you don't talk about?"

She wrapped her arms around herself. "Yes."

"Is he still living? Is there hope for reconciliation between you?"

"As far as I know, he's still alive." She pursed her lips. "But he's not like you. Reconciliation is not possible."

"That makes me sad."

Her eyes jerked to his.

"Sad for you." He scuffed the toe of his boot against the porch step. "I'm not sure which is harder, forgiving ourselves or those who've hurt us. I'm working on both."

"Have I told you how much I admire the man you've become, Nathan Crenshaw?"

A whisper of something startling, like the wing of a blue jay in flight, flitted across his gaze.

"You make me want to be better." A muscle ticked in his jaw. "To believe there could be more. For the boys." His cheeks beneath the beard stubble reddened. "For myself."

Her heart hammered. Fifteen years ago, Nathan had been crystal clear about his feelings and intentions. Over the last few weeks, however, he'd been the master of mixed signals. Was he implying—

He moved to the steps. "I'd best talk to Kody."

She wasn't sure what he said to Kody. They were in his room a long time. When they emerged, both man and boy looked a little worse for wear. Their eyes appeared red-rimmed, but from the way Kody held on to his father's hand, restoration had occurred.

Kody apologized to her. She hugged the little boy and told him not to worry about it anymore. Ike, Rascal and Connor drifted into the house.

It had been a fun, busy weekend. Too busy. Her emotions felt raw and wrung out.

Tomorrow would be Ike's first foray back to church. But she couldn't help but dread what the notorious Truelove grapevine would have to say about what happened on the square today.

Chapter Thirteen

That night, Nate fell asleep almost immediately, but his sleep was interrupted with fragmented, random dreams of the sweet spring Connor was born. He and Deanna had been young and unsure of themselves but so in love with the little boy God had given them. In the confusing way of dreams, one minute he and Deanna were delighting in Connor's first steps and the next, the dream segued to Deanna, getting into her car that final day.

Gasping for breath, pulse jumping wildly, he awoke with an ache so intense in his chest, for a minute he wondered if he was having a heart attack. When his breathing slowed and the strange ache faded, he rolled out of the bed, knowing further sleep was impossible.

Pulling on his work clothes and donning his coat, he slipped out of the house earlier than usual to do his chores. Pushing the dream aside, he took comfort in the taxing physical labor.

Returning to the house, he was surprised to find his father staring out the kitchen window and drinking coffee. Rascal thumped his tail on the floor. Toeing out of his boots, Nate shot a look at the carafe of coffee. He hadn't thought to get it going before he left the house. After what happened with the soup...

His dad raised his mug. "Gemma made the coffee, not me."

Nate's gaze darted, but his father was alone in the kitchen.

"She's getting ready for church. The boys, too."

Nate poured himself a cup of coffee. He sank into a chair.

"Everything all right with you, son?"

"I'm thinking the heifer will calve sometime over the next few weeks." Nate lifted the mug to his lips. "The wind has shifted. Temps are on the rise. The boys will be disappointed to see the snow melt."

"First day of December." His dad's mouth curved. "No need to get in a lather about snow. There'll be more, lots more, before the daffodils bloom in spring. But I wasn't asking about the ranch or the weather. You seem subdued."

He shrugged. "Didn't sleep well last night."

"Something troubling your mind?"

Too much on his mind. None of which he wanted to delve into with his father.

"I'll be fine once I get some caffeine in my system."

His dad set down his coffee cup. "If you're worried about me with Rascal at church today, you and Gemma cleared it with Pastor Bryant this week, right?"

"Pastor Bryant has no issues with Rascal. He was thrilled you'd be able to worship with the church family again."

"Is it just thoughts of me in general keeping you up at night, son?" His father laid his hand over Nate's. "I worry what this disease is doing to you, too."

Nate squeezed his hand. "Last night wasn't about you, Dad. I kept having this dream over and over…"

"About?"

"It was weird. One minute Deanna and I are just married, then Connor is born and the next minute we're both older and she gets into the Jeep…" He turned his face away. "I don't know why all of a sudden I'm dreaming about that again."

His father sat back. "I could hazard a guess."

Nate stiffened. "Not everything is about Gemma, Dad."

"I didn't say it was, but I do wonder if God sent her into

our lives not just for me, but also as a catalyst to help you face your loss once and for all."

"It's been two years. I've put all that behind me and got on with my life."

"Have you?" His father looked at him. "Take it from a guy who's been widowed longer than your mother and I were married. Missing someone doesn't ever completely go away. And that's okay. That's the price we pay for loving and being loved in return."

He glared at his father. "I'm not having this conversation with you about Deanna."

"It would do you a world of good to talk about her. If not to me, then someone. Your sons are confused by your silence on the topic of their mother. They need to hear you speak about Deanna almost as much as you need to talk about her. Keeping her locked inside your heart isn't healthy for anyone."

Nate scraped back his chair. Rascal raised his head. "The usual over-easy egg for you, Dad?"

"It's no surprise to me this is cropping up in your dreams. You've never let yourself grieve properly. Often the subconscious will force you to acknowledge in the darkness what the conscious mind refuses to deal with in the daylight."

He scowled at his dad. Why wouldn't his father let this go? "Every time I think about her, much less talk about her, I feel like I'm the one dying." He pinched the bridge of his nose. "Don't you see, Dad? I can't… Once I open the floodgates, I'll drown."

"You're drowning now, son." Sorrow clouded his father's features. "Once you open the floodgates, I think that is when you'll finally reach the surface."

He stared at his father. Was he right? Instead of hiding from the pain, was the only way forward to face it?

Kody stumbled into the kitchen. "What's for bweakfast?" His son winked sleep from his eyes.

Nate's gaze pinged from his father to his son. His heart lurched. In refusing to talk about their mother, he'd thought to spare his sons. But was it them he was really trying to spare or himself? His dad dropped his head and Nate realized he was praying. For him.

The whisper of a memory floated through his mind. Of Deanna, her bouncing blond curls, and the love in her sparkling eyes when she looked at her youngest, most rambunctious son, Kody.

And at him.

"How about pancakes, Kode?" He swallowed. "With chocolate chip eyes and a mouth just like Mom used to make you?"

Kody stilled. "Mommy made me chocolate-face pancakes?"

"Every Sunday morning before church." Connor wandered in behind his brother. "Right, Dad?"

He smiled. "That's right."

"I 'member that, Connor." Kody pulled at his brother's arm. "I really 'member."

Kneeling in front of his boys, he gathered his sons in his arms. *God, forgive me. Help me to do better by them and by Deanna.* The boys helped him put together the pancakes. Bellies full, they were sitting around the table later when Gemma hurried into the kitchen.

"Something smells delicious. Am I too late?"

"Not too late." Nate took in the soft glow in her cheeks and the russet ribbon tied at the end of her single braid. "You're just in time."

In more ways than one?

Something this morning felt different about Nathan, but for the life of her, Gemma couldn't quite pinpoint what it was. But she sensed something within him had shifted. He was quiet as ever, but there was a peaceful quality to his gaze that hadn't been there yesterday.

When he'd looked at her in the kitchen this morning…she'd felt… She wasn't sure what she felt.

In the graveled church parking lot, she got out of the truck. Afraid to give voice to the emotions that filled her every time she looked at him, she took in her surroundings instead. Nestled in a glade on the edge of town, the black church steeple brushed a picture-perfect Blue Ridge sky. She followed the Crenshaws over a tiny footbridge, which spanned a small creek. Water trickled over moss-covered stones.

Patches of melted snow dotted the glossy green leaves of the camellia bushes around the entrance. The boys hurried off to children's church in the education wing. Ike and Rascal led the way into the white clapboard church. A slight tension between her shoulder blades, she and Nathan followed him into the sanctuary.

This was the last big hurdle for Rascal in restoring to Ike a semblance of his previously independent and vibrant social life. Pastor Bryant had been so accommodating on the phone. He'd sent out a special church-wide email to members, explaining the protocols that should be observed with an assistance dog on Sunday mornings.

Inside the foyer, Ike strode confidently ahead to a side pew near the back that Reverend Bryant had set aside for him. It had the benefit of being close to the exit should Ike feel the need to a sudden, unobtrusive departure.

She need not have worried about the congregation. Old friends greeted him but left Rascal to do his duty. Ike fairly beamed at the prospect of being back in the Truelove fold once again.

The music from the organ swelled. Nathan gestured for her to take her seat first. She became aware of significant glances thrown her way and Nathan's. That the two of them together represented a topic of great interest did not escape her notice. Not that they were together, of course.

But the service began and she let herself soak in the ambience of the two-hundred-year-old sanctuary. Wide-planked beams soared overhead and prisms of light shone through the stained glass windows onto the gleaming brass cross on the altar.

After a brief, but powerfully reflective sermon, Reverend Bryant said a benediction and everyone dispersed to the fellowship hall for Christmas cookies and hot apple cider.

To her surprise, Shayla made an effort to seek her out. "I was wondering if you'd meet me for coffee sometime this week."

"I would love that. Let me check with Tom to see when the ROMEOs are getting together. The boys will be in school. What about your little guy?"

"Luke's mom is always ready to Jeremiah-sit. I could drop him off at her house and meet you at the Jar."

They made tentative plans to coordinate their schedules. But the next day, Shayla called to beg off due to Jeremiah developing a fussy cold. They rescheduled. But as it turned out, the day they chose was the same day as Connor's winter wonderland production at the elementary school. He had a speaking part, which she rehearsed over and over with him. One line, but he was nervous. He asked her to go and she would as soon miss his performance as cut off her arm. Sitting in the audience between Ike and Nathan, she couldn't have been more proud of him if he were her own.

She was a bit embarrassed canceling on Shayla but the singer insisted they put another date on the calendar closer to Christmas.

Over the next few weeks, there was lots of pre-Christmas fun. Including teaching the boys to decorate sugar cookies. Nathan got into the merriment. Ike got into the eating.

They were the best weeks of her life. A permanent caregiver wasn't set to arrive until after the New Year.

She couldn't wait for Christmas. Yet at the same time, she never wanted this time with Nathan and his family to end.

About a week before Christmas, Nate was getting an early start on gathering receipts to pay his quarterly taxes in January. Looking troubled, Gemma came into his office. "I'm sorry to interrupt."

"I'm working on taxes." He leaned back. "Please interrupt."

She fingered the red silk ribbon in her braid. A nervous habit, he'd noticed. A habit that never failed to play havoc with his nerve endings. "You've probably already taken care of this, but I noticed there were no presents under the tree for the boys."

He rubbed his chin. "I've been meaning to go shopping. I've ordered a few things online, but haven't gotten around to wrapping them."

"I'd be glad to do that for you, if you'd like."

"Thank you." He sighed. "I'm a complete failure in the dad department, aren't I?"

She shook her head. "Not in any way that actually matters."

"There's still several things I'd hoped to buy the boys and Dad, too, but that would involve a mall." He shuddered. "Which involves heading to Asheville. I'm pretty hopeless at shopping period."

"Greensboro has a mall." She fiddled with the small gold cross at her neck. "I hate to ask for time off, but the Spencers left for Virginia last week and Ma got a message a package had been left on the porch."

"You are doing us a tremendous favor by looking after Dad until New Year's." He leaned his elbows on the desk. "You are due more than a single day off."

"If I leave first thing tomorrow morning, I'll be back before bedtime. Maggie asked CoraFaye Dolan to sit with him while I'm away."

He smiled. "Cousin CoraFaye is a firecracker. She'll keep him on the straight and narrow." His smile fell. "That's a long way to go—three hours?—to put a package inside a house. Isn't there a neighbor who could—"

"Ma didn't ask. I offered. The Spencers have done so much for me."

He looked at her, willing her to open up to him if only a little.

She took a breath. "After my mother died, I lived with them for several years while I took classes at the community college."

"You lived with them because you and your father are estranged. They adopted you?"

Immediately, her expression closed and he realized he'd pushed too far.

"I'd like to check on my apartment, too. If you give me a list, I'd be happy to do your shopping." She batted her lashes at him. "I'm real good when it comes to spending other people's money."

He wasn't fooled by her deflection, but he let it go. "Not that I don't trust you with my money…" He smiled to take the sting out of his words.

She laughed.

"But six hours of driving is a lot in one day." He steepled his hands under his chin. "I wouldn't mind a minivacation from the ranch myself. What would you think about me tagging along and doing the driving?" He held his breath, certain she'd refuse. She was such a private person.

"If you're sure you can spare the time…?" She gave him a pleased, shy smile. "I'd like that."

He felt like he'd just hung the moon. "Christmas road trip, here we come."

The boys were distraught they had to go to school and miss the fun.

With a knowing look in his eyes, which Nate did his best to ignore, his dad chuckled. "There's kid fun and then there's young-folk fun. I'm sure your dad and Gemma won't get up to much trouble." He winked. Gemma went scarlet. He glared at his father.

Bright and early the next morning, they got into his truck.

She tossed her braid over her shoulder. "My first time riding shotgun in your truck."

He grinned. "How's it feel?"

She waggled her shoulders. "Great."

"You look great."

Her eyes flitted to his. It was true. Riding beside him in the truck, she looked more than great. Beautiful.

They stopped at the bakery for coffee and pastries to go. The time flew by. They laughed and chatted and talked about everything under the sun.

Before he knew it, he was pulling into Laurel Grove. It was a pretty town. "You going to give me the grand tour?"

"Hardly grand." She rolled her eyes. "A ten-cent tour will suffice and you'll have change left over. I forgot you've never been here."

"Juliet and I videoconferenced most of our business regarding Rascal." He drove around the town square. "Reminds me a lot of Truelove."

They rode up and down Main Street. She pointed out the knit shop owned by Juliet's mom.

"Ewe Made Me Luv You." He laughed. "I love it."

She pointed out the PawPals office building. She directed him to a suburban section not far from downtown. When he pulled into the driveway of a small midcentury modern brick house, she hopped out of the truck. She tucked the brown parcel inside the house and clambered back into the truck.

"Where to now, boss lady?"

"Since when did I become the boss lady?"

He grinned. "Since you became my personal shopper."

They headed to Greensboro. They hit the mall first. He was amazed at how easily she secured the items on his list. Found a lot of bargains, too. She even made a few suggestions for gifts he hadn't thought about buying for the boys.

By lunchtime, his Christmas shopping was done for another year. She took him to one of her favorite places for a late lunch, a locally famous Mexican restaurant. They went to her apartment. No photos of family. But a lot of dog paraphernalia. She gave him a tour of Greensboro. Despite the cold, they had ice cream. It was one of the most perfect days he could remember—just spending time with her.

Sitting in his truck, she straightened. "I didn't realize how dark it had gotten. We should probably head back to Truelove."

He shrugged. "Kind of hate for the day to end." He looked at her.

"I hate for the day to end, too." She looked down and then up at him. "There's one more place I'd like to show you if wouldn't mind another detour. One of my favorite places this time of year in Greensboro, but it is at its best when seen at night."

He cocked his head. "That's intriguing."

She fluttered her hands. "Totally worth the wait, I promise."

Like Gemma herself? His heart thudded.

"There's this neighborhood—Sunset Hills—they started the tradition to collect cans for the food bank, but more and more houses got involved until now…" She smiled. "Well, you'll see. It's better than any theme park or light show. It's magical, especially with snow on the ground."

What was magical was the sweet, childlike look on her face as she described the multicolored, illuminated Christmas balls the neighbors hung from trees with the aid of a potato launcher. She gave him directions. It was a short drive.

Her description failed to do justice to the spectacle before him.

"Wow," he rasped.

She grinned at him. "I told you."

They drove through the neighborhood for a while. He pulled over to an empty parking space along the curb, out of the way of the line of cars snaking through the subdivision, also taking in the sights.

"Want to get out and stretch our legs before the long journey home?"

For a second, her eyes watered. He wondered if she might cry, but he had no idea why. "I'd love, that, Nathan." Her voice had gone small. "So much."

Him, too. Anything to prolong their time together. Getting out of the truck, she tucked her hand in the crook of his elbow and they wandered down the block until they found a relatively deserted spot under a gigantic oak, heavy with blue-and-white illuminated Christmas globes. Looking out over the illuminated neighborhood, her eyes shone.

"I wished you could always look as happy as you do now," he rasped.

She turned to him. "I wish that for you, too, Nathan."

With her, suddenly he felt it possible. But what about Deanna? How could he make her understand?

"I wasn't always a great husband to Deanna."

Her posture tensed. "What do you mean?"

"Too often, I was emotionally unavailable. It wasn't fair to her. I have a difficult time expressing my emotions. I prefer to bury them. I've found it less painful."

Her mouth quivered. "How much of that is my fault?"

"Not all of it. It's how I coped when my mother died and after Deanna…" He swallowed. "But it's hard. I want to talk about her with you. I need to talk about her, but I…" His throat closed.

"There's no rush." Her hands cupped his face. "Whenever you're ready."

His heart leaped. *God, this time could they make it work?*

The distance between them had lessened. He had only to bend his head. Their lips were a mere fraction apart. But kissing her again—this, them—was a bad, bad idea. Yet he could no more deny her than he could deny his desperate need to hold her in his arms. If only once more. He drew her closer into the circle of his arms.

Her face upturned to his, her lips parted. "Nathan…"

Nate's heart turned over in his chest. He wrapped a tendril of her hair around his finger, and her hair was as he remembered. Like spun gold.

The pain of the past fell away. The uncertainty of the future didn't exist. All that mattered was that she was in his arms. She felt so good in his arms. So right. Like she'd always belonged. And nothing that had gone before mattered.

She lifted her face to his. He lowered his head. Only a hairbreadth separated them. Their breath mingled in the frosty air.

Gently he brushed his lips across her cheek. Then his mouth drifted to hers. When he would have pulled away, she cradled his face in the palms of her hands and kissed him back.

There was a rightness in her kiss. An undeniable truth. As inexorable as the moon rising over the mountain. Kissing her felt like coming home.

But his doubts, his fears, and his guilt remained an ever-present reminder of why a future with Gemma might never be possible.

Chapter Fourteen

It was late when they returned to Truelove. Yet in the days that followed, Gemma felt so hopeful. Nathan wasn't the kind of man who would have kissed her like that unless he was falling in love. He was also starting to open up to her about his late wife.

Christmas and the New Year felt bright with possibilities.

On the afternoon of the twenty-third, Gemma left the ranch for her coffee get-together with Shayla.

Nathan practically ushered her out of the house. "No need to hurry back."

Ike waved from the porch. "We've got plenty to keep us occupied."

She propped her hands on her hips. "What are you guys up to?"

Kody dissolved in a fit of giggles. "You're gonna be surprised at what's under the tree."

Connor glared at his little brother. "Hush, Kode. It's supposed to be a secret."

From the tape dispenser and scissors left on the kitchen island, she suspected an afternoon of gift wrapping was about to commence on her behalf.

"I'm sure whatever you do, I'll love it." Smiling, she got into her car. She didn't need presents. Observing their joy when they opened their packages on Christmas morning would be gift enough.

At the Jar, she found Shayla waiting for her. Settling against the blue upholstery of the booth, Shayla smiled and folded her hands in her lap. "Tell me about yourself."

From long practice, it was a question easily dodged. She spent a full five minutes chatting about the Crenshaws and her work at PawPals. A waitress brought their drinks.

Gemma wrapped her hands around the steaming white porcelain mug. "What about you?" A Christmas aroma of cloves and nutmeg filled her nostrils.

As she talked about her son and her husband, Shayla's eyes took on an added luster. The Truelove songbird was refreshingly down-to-earth.

"I feel so honored you made time for coffee with me."

A glimmer of uncertainty flickered across Shayla's gaze. "At the open house…there was something about the way you held yourself that reminded me of… I felt I should get to know you better."

Unsure what to make of that, Gemma changed topics. "Any upcoming platinum selling song of yours I should be on the lookout for?"

Shayla took a sip of her peppermint-spiced concoction. "I've written a new song for the Christmas Eve candlelight service. I hope people will like it."

"Don't tell me *the* Shayla Morgan gets nervous."

"I wasn't always Shayla Morgan." She shrugged. "I come from a run-down trailer park on the other side of the river. My family are locally notorious ne'er-do-wells."

Cup halfway to her lips, Gemma stilled.

Shayla gave her a brittle smile. "When I was a little girl, my mother walked away without a backward look. In and out of prison, my father and brothers specialize in grand theft auto."

Gemma put down her mug. "I had no idea. Seeing you at the tree farm with Luke and Jeremiah—"

"My life is wonderful, but it wasn't always so."

"How did you…?" Gemma stopped.

"How did I overcome the shame of the past and get to where I am now?"

Gemma dropped her gaze to the tabletop. "It's none of my business."

"At first, I made a lot of bad decisions. Trying to outrun my past—which never works—I jumped out of the frying pan into the fire with Jeremiah's abusive, drug-dealing father."

Gemma looked at her.

Shayla fingered the handle on her cup. "In every way that matters, Luke is Jeremiah's dad, but he isn't his biological father."

"I… I didn't realize."

Uncharacteristically, she found herself wanting to share her family background with Shayla. With someone who might actually understand where she was coming from. Who might give her hope beyond the web of shame in which she was entangled.

"Where I'm from—Laurel Grove, a small, rural town—my father is notorious, too." She locked eyes with Shayla to gauge her reaction. "He's serving life without parole for murdering my mother and a law enforcement officer."

Shayla laid her hand on top of Gemma's. "I'm so sorry."

"My childhood…" She bit her lip. "My father was violent. We were constantly on tenterhooks to please him. We never knew what would trigger his rage."

Shayla nodded. "It's a hard way to live. And confusing. Especially for a child."

"I learned early not to trust men. One minute he'd be warm and charming. The next?" She clenched her fists. "He could—and still does—turn on a smile at the drop of a hat. Most of the time, I never saw the hit coming."

"Your mother didn't report him to the police?"

Gemma looked at her. "He was the police. The chief of police."

Shayla put her hand to her throat. "Oh."

"His public image was everything to him. Neither my mother or I ever said a word about what went on within the four walls of our home. Weird, isn't it, how we kept his secrets? A conspiracy of enabling silence."

Shayla shook her head. "My father's abuse took the form of neglect. Though several loving adults in my life tried to intervene on my behalf, I would've died before telling them the truth. Children in our situation are conditioned from birth to protect the dysfunction we know."

"I believed it was normal." Gemma pressed her lips together. "I believed I deserved it. Until recently, I was angry at my mother for refusing to leave him, forcing me to endure it, too. But now I understand how over the years he'd worn her down. To believe she was nothing and powerless. Robbing her of hope."

Shayla squeezed her hand. "That was my greatest challenge— to overcome the worthlessness I felt. It was only when I became pregnant with Jeremiah I found the courage to leave. Because my baby deserved better. How did your family situation go unnoticed?"

"My father is clever and manipulative. The psych eval after the fact diagnosed him as a narcissist with sociopathic tendencies. No excuse, but apparently, his own childhood was less than stellar, too. No one ever suspected the truth until that last, fatal day."

Shayla sighed. "I understand if you don't want to talk about it, but I'm here for you if you do."

"At the time, it was front-page news." She knotted her hands. "Outside Laurel Grove, most people have forgotten, but it's the reason I never settled there. In an effort to live down his notoriety, I changed my last name."

"The Spencers aren't your family?"

Gemma took a deep breath. "On the tiny Laurel Grove police force, Pa Spencer was second-in-command. He and his wife took me in after what happened. I think he felt he owed me for not seeing what was right under his nose. For not doing something until it was far, far too late."

Shayla fingered the handle of her mug. "Laurel Grove is near Greensboro?"

Gemma nodded. "There are a group of older ladies in Laurel Grove—the Knit-Knack Club—who remind me of the Double Name Club. They chair every church committee, fundraiser or festival. My father demanded community participation to make him look good. He didn't allow Mom to have friends, but I think they suspected the truth. Garden of the year. Quilt shows. Unable to get her to leave him, they supported her the best way they could—by making sure she always won."

"What about you?"

"His expectations were impossible to meet, but I excelled at school sports. I tried to project the confident, self-assured Gemma on the outside I most definitely was not on the inside. I became adept at hiding the real me."

Toying with a sugar packet, she told Shayla about joining the 4-H Club in Laurel Grove.

"I always loved animals. The summer after my junior year, Juliet and I were hired as camp counselors for the regional 4-H camp, located a couple of hours west. Mama knew how badly I wanted to go. Behind my father's back, she helped me fill out the job application. It was understood he would never let me go."

"But you went anyway."

"I'm not sure how she managed it. I never stopped to consider what she must've suffered once I set off with Juliet. The small act of defiance would've cost her dearly. But if only for a summer, I escaped his clutches."

"Camp is where you met Nate?"

Gemma smiled. "It was the most wonderful summer of my life."

"You fell in love?"

"I never fell out." She sighed. "He was so different from my father. Kind, gentle. And good."

"What happened to separate you and Nate?"

"At summer's end, I had to go home, but I'd hoped… I'd hoped…" For a second, she squeezed her eyes shut. "Instead, I walked into the house to find my father waiting. His anger had an entire summer to fester."

Gemma gazed out the window overlooking the Truelove green, grounding herself in the present and away from the life-altering moment she returned to Laurel Grove. "This time his rage had no words. And that was the most terrifying thing of all."

Shayla's mouth quivered.

"He pulled his service revolver. Mama told me to run to my bedroom and lock the door." Her breath came quick, short and uneven. "If only I hadn't left her to face him alone."

Shayla grabbed her hand. "You would've been dead, too."

"I ran. Slammed the door behind me. Locked it. Barricaded it with every piece of furniture I could shove against it. My father, the master of control, lost it. Lost it completely. Mama got between him and my door."

A single tear cascaded down Shayla's cheek. Her lips moved, but no words emerged. Gemma knew she was praying for her. Praying for her to be able to tell the rest of the story.

"He shot Mama." Saying the words made her stomach roil. "He was doing his best to batter down my bedroom door when Pa Spencer and the patrol officer on duty arrived. The officer's wife was expecting their first child. He'd only been on the force a few months. He tried to stop my father. My father killed him, too. While he was distracted, Pa Spencer was able to immobilize him."

"Does Nate know what happened?"

She shook her head. "You know the kind of man he is. The sort of family he comes from. How could I bring my garbage into his life?"

"You weren't to blame for the choices your father made, Gemma."

"But I am to blame for the choices I made. It's because I went to camp my mother died." She opened her hands. "How could I be with Nathan? Knowing my happy life with him cost my mother hers?"

"Because she would've wanted you to be happy." Shayla clutched her arm. "Only God can help you work through the feelings of unworthiness. To answer your question about how I overcame the stigma of my circumstances...?"

Gemma glanced up.

"I made a distinct break from the past. Jeremiah's birth was the catalyst that ended that chapter of my life."

Gemma considered her words. "For me, I think the catalyst was the therapy dog the Spencers adopted to help me work through the trauma I'd experienced. It was because of the difference the little Cavalier made for me, I became a K-9 trainer."

Shayla nodded. "You stopped being a victim and became an advocate on behalf of others."

"I never looked at it that way, but that's exactly what happened."

"Marking a break with the past doesn't make the past disappear, nor should it." Shayla leaned forward. "The past is a part of you. Your new identity can only take hold if a new path forward emerges from the ashes of the old."

Gemma tilted her head. "Ultimately, the darkness led me to a fulfilling career with Juliet at PawPals."

"For obvious reasons, you find it difficult to share your feelings about what happened. But not talking about challenging emotions serves no purpose other than keeping you stuck in the past." Shayla waved her hands. "An emotional paralysis."

Her thoughts flew to Nathan and his difficulty in talking about Deanna.

"Every time I find the courage to share my story with someone, I work through more of the negative emotions. I am far more than the unloved, neglected child I was or a man's punching bag." Shayla lifted her chin. "I am a musician. A wife. A mother. A lot of people love me. I refuse to remain defined by my family's estimation."

A lot of people loved Gemma, too. Although until now, she hadn't stopped to consider how many. Juliet, her mom—Lesley—the Knit-Knack Club, Ma and Pa Spencer.

"Don't allow your father's warped perspective to hold you forever in its grip." Shayla laid her palms flat on the tabletop. "You can't break the cycle until you accept who you are and what was done to you. No one moves forward until they forgive themselves. If you don't, you condemn yourself to a lifetime of guilt and shame."

Shayla locked eyes with Gemma. "The sad, scared little girl from the trailer park deserves better than that. And so do you, my friend. So do you."

For the first time in her life, Gemma found herself believing it. "You've given me much to think about." She bit her lip. "And pray about, too."

"If you ever need to talk, I'm here for you."

"Thank you, Shayla. For everything." She glanced at the clock on the wall. "I need to get back to the ranch to check on Ike." She eased out of the booth.

Shayla rose. "Secrets take on a life of their own. I came close to losing the beautiful future God had waiting for me with Luke." She gripped Gemma's coat. "No matter how ugly it is, we owe the ones we love the truth. Tell Nate what happened before it's too late."

"I will," she promised.

Driving toward the ranch, she thanked God for Shayla's willingness to be vulnerable with someone she barely knew. Maybe one day, Gemma could do the same for someone else.

How would Nathan react to learning the truth about her past? Once he learned what had happened, would he reject her and the possibility of a future together?

Veering into the long graveled drive of the High Country Ranch, she prayed for courage to speak the truth to him. And most of all, for him to be able to receive it.

Gemma had every intention of finding a quiet moment alone with Nathan to finally explain why she'd ended their relationship, but instead she walked into an unexpected Christmas crisis.

She gaped at Nate. "Ike did what?"

Leaning against the kitchen counter, he folded his arms. "Dad signed us up to participate in the church's Living Nativity tonight."

She shrugged. "Okay…"

Nate shot a dark glance at his father, sitting with Rascal at the kitchen table. "I don't think you fully appreciate the dilemma in which we find ourselves. It's a costumed event."

His dad smiled. "It'll be fun."

Seated on a stool, Connor rested his elbows on the island. "Who are we supposed to be?"

Beside his brother, Kody swung his legs. "I want to be a camel."

"You and Connor are shepherd boys." Nate grimaced. "If Reverend Bryant hadn't called to check on us after we didn't attend the dress rehearsal, the entire pageant would've been ruined when we didn't show up tonight. Why didn't you tell me, Dad?"

A stricken look on his face, his father scratched his head. "I wanted to make a memory as a family. But since I couldn't even remember to tell you about it, I guess I'm not much of a wise man."

"You are a wise man, costume or not. Dementia or not." Lips pursed, she crossed the kitchen to stand behind his dad's chair. "I think it's a wonderful idea. But having missed the dress rehearsal, is this still doable?"

His father nodded. "They use the same costumes every year. No need for special fittings." He hung his head. "I'm sorry, Nate."

She put her hand on his shoulder. "Are there lines to be memorized?"

His dad shook his head. "They play Christmas carols from the loudspeakers. Everybody in the nativity scene just stands there and looks authentic."

She threw Nate a pointed look. "Then I see no reason the Crenshaw family can't give Ike his Christmas wish, do you?"

He scrubbed his face with his hand. "When you put it like that…"

"Yay!" Kody fist-pumped the air. "Can I be the little dwummer boy?"

"No!" Connor and Nate said at the same time.

Kody frowned. "Will there be sheep?"

His father smiled. "One for each of you."

The boys grinned. "Cool!"

She arched her eyebrow. "And what is your role, Nathan?"

He rubbed at the kinks in his neck. "Dad signed me and Tom up to be the other wise men."

"A Stetson-wearing wise man." She smirked. "Are you in charge of the gold, silver or myrrh?"

"Laugh it up." He cocked his head. "But we aren't the only

ones making a command performance. You'll be the most dazzling Christmas angel the Truelove Living Nativity has ever seen."

She blinked rapidly. "An angel?"

Nate grinned. "Dad also promised one of the heifers and Rascal, too."

His father chuckled. "What would a stable be without animals?"

At the church that evening, under the supervision of his great-aunt GeorgeAnne, they donned their costumes and took their places.

Like the pinpricks of diamonds on a field of black velvet, stars studded the night sky. Sam and Lila Gibson, with their five-month-old son, Asher, were the principal players in this year's Living Nativity. People from as far away as Boone and Asheville arrived for the cherished Truelove tradition.

However, when he realized he had to stand still and not speak for the duration of their shift, Kody became less enthused. But averting a potential shepherd mutiny, Gemma assured him she knew he could do it and told him how proud she was of him.

His breath fogging in the chilly air, Nate looked with love and pride over the little tableau of his family. As for Gemma?

Dressed in a flowing white costume and bedecked with golden wings, she was positioned on a small balcony overlooking the manger scene below. He hadn't been kidding earlier when he told her she would be the most beautiful Christmas angel Truelove had ever seen.

She was all that and then some.

He'd never seen her hair out of the single braid she favored. But tonight it hung loose and crinkly, waving about her shoulders. She took his breath away. But she'd been doing that since he first laid eyes on her so long ago.

Nate's heart turned over in his chest. She was so lovely, inside and out. Standing under the brilliance of the Christmas balls in Greensboro, it hadn't been easy talking about Deanna. He'd hoped it might spark a reciprocal conversation about why she'd ended things between them.

Yet even after he'd bared his feelings in the aftermath of Deanna's death, Gemma held tightly to her own secrets. Leaving him more confused than ever that pursuing a relationship with her was the right thing. For the boys. For himself.

The Living Nativity ended soon after eight o'clock. Everyone congratulated the boys on their portrayals. Gemma's eyes sparkled. It was all he could do not to take her into his arms and announce his growing feelings for her to the world. But he didn't. He couldn't. Not with secrets between them.

The next day was Christmas Eve. Several times, he sensed Gemma maneuvering to have a private moment together. But beset with his own doubts, he took care to avoid being alone with her.

Late afternoon, he and Connor tromped out to the pasture to check on the heifer about to calve.

"How much longer, Daddy? Maybe a Christmas Eve calf?"

"No sign the cow's in labor yet." He slung his arm around his eldest son's shoulders. "We'll check on her again when we return from the candlelight service tonight. In the meantime, let's roll out hay in case she needs a warm, dry place to lie down."

Later at the church, with dozens of lighted candles in the windows lining the walls of the sanctuary, the service was especially beautiful. When they returned to the ranch, his dad, Gemma and the boys decided to help him check on the heifer. They left Rascal inside the house.

He spotted the black heifer sprawled on her side in the bed of hay he and Connor laid down earlier. By the time they reached her, the heifer was pushing for all she was worth.

"We're just in time." Connor gasped. "I already see the calf's front feet and a nose, Daddy."

"Hang back, guys." He put his hand on Kody to stop him from rushing forward. "Keep your voices down. Let her do her thing."

Gemma stood close to his elbow. "Shouldn't we do something?"

He shook his head. "As long as she isn't having trouble, it's better for her to calve on her own. We'll stand by in case she has difficulty getting up afterward to mother her calf."

"The birthing doesn't take long," his dad assured her.

Immediately after the delivery, the heifer began to lick her calf.

Ike crouched between the boys. "If a calf doesn't get up right away, it runs the risk of death due to cold or dehydration."

Nate smiled at his father, happy to see him in his true element again, a proud cattle rancher. Within five minutes, the calf was standing.

A sheen of happy tears shone in Gemma's eyes. "God's creation is so amazing and precious."

Like love.

He slipped his hand into hers. Leaning into him, she squeezed his fingers. Tonight, everything in his world felt so right. So perfect. So meant to be.

Something long numb in his heart blazed to life. Gemma got it. She got the ranching life. She got him. He put away his fears for the future to relish the here and now.

It was late by the time they were able to tear the boys away from Mistletoe the calf and his mother. Yet the boys were awake before the crack of dawn, eager to dive into opening the presents under the Christmas tree.

Full of their usual high spirits, they ripped off the paper Gemma had so painstakingly wrapped for them. They oohed and aahed over the gifts she'd helped him select.

Bleary-eyed from lack of sleep, he got as much enjoyment out of watching her animated face as in his sons tearing open their gifts.

She declared herself enchanted with the presents the boys had clumsily wrapped for her. Rascal had gifts, which Kody out of the kindness of his heart offered to open for the collie.

Connor threw his brother an exaggerated eye roll.

There was also a present for Mistletoe. Nate had tucked the gift away in case the calf made an appearance for Christmas. Sir Hops-a-Lot and Hare-i-et were not forgotten, either.

Sipping coffee, he was about to talk to Gemma about what he'd been feeling over the last few days, when his phone—lying on the kitchen table between them—buzzed.

It wasn't a number he immediately recognized. "Hello?"

Just like that, everything changed.

Chapter Fifteen

It was the woman from the agency regarding a permanent caregiver for his dad.

As he clutched the phone to his ear, Nate's gaze cut to Gemma.

Beside him at the kitchen table, she touched his arm. "What is it?" she whispered.

He spoke into the phone. "When?" His eyebrows rose. "That's…that's…" His voice hitched. "That's good news."

But his gut tanked.

"Nathan?"

With a slight shake of his head, he listened as the agency lady gave details about when to expect Mrs. Jewell. His mind racing, he thanked the lady and clicked off. Nate stared at the phone in his hand.

Silence ticked between him and Gemma.

"Tell me."

He laid his cell on the table. "Because of the urgency of our situation, even though it's Christmas day, the lady at the agency called to let me know a permanent caregiver has become available sooner than expected."

"When?"

"I hoped we'd have until the New Year." He took a breath. "Mrs. Jewell will arrive first thing tomorrow morning."

She went still. Too still. She looked at him. "What does this mean?"

He plowed his hand through his hair. "I don't know what it will mean."

"What do you want it to mean?"

"Things will have to change." He dropped his gaze to the table. "Dad will have to adjust to a new caregiver."

"I meant what do you want it to mean for us?"

Nate scrubbed his hand over his face. "I don't know."

"I think you do know."

He looked at her. "I thought I'd have more time to…"

"To what?"

He heaved a sigh. "To come to terms with the past."

"I should've explained long before now why I ended things between us. I meant to but—"

He walked over to peer out the window over the sink. "How can there be an 'us' when you can't bring yourself to tell me what you were thinking and feeling then, much less now?"

Jumping up, she hurried to his side. "I want to tell you. I need to tell you."

She told him what happened the day she got home from camp. He stared at her in horror at what she'd endured.

"I never suspected…" His throat went tight. "You never said anything that summer about your father."

Tears filled her eyes. "It was hard to talk about. It's still hard to talk about."

He touched her arm. "I'm sorry you lost your mom that way. Why didn't you tell me, Gemma? Why the voicemail?"

"After it happened, I wasn't in a good place. I was a mess. I was consumed with shame and self-loathing."

Placing his hands on her shoulders, he turned her to face him. "Nothing about what happened was your fault."

She took a shuddery breath. "It took a long time to get my head straight. A lot of love to heal from the trauma."

He shook his head. "I would've been there for you. I wanted

nothing more than to be with you. I could have been the one to love you back to recovery."

"For a long time, guilt and my love for you were mixed up in my head." She put her arms around him. "But not anymore."

Guilt and love? He stiffened. *Deanna...*

"Forgive me, Nathan." She pressed her cheek against his shirt. "Forgive me for failing you."

He clamped his jaw tight. "There's nothing to forgive."

"We can move forward from here." She lifted her head. "The time wasn't right then for us, but now..."

Move forward? The ache in his chest intensified, becoming nearly unbearable. Sweat broke out on his brow.

She peered at him. "What are you thinking? Talk to me."

Nate felt at a point of no return. He couldn't do this again. Risk falling into an infinite abyss of hurt with Gemma like the last time.

He pushed her away. She staggered. "I... I can't. There's Dad's illness and the boys to consider. I told you from the beginning I wasn't in a position to pursue a long-term relationship. We agreed there'd be no expectations. No promises."

Nate's head throbbed. His heart hurt. He raised his hand to his forehead only to realize it was shaking. He dropped his hand to his side.

"We don't have to return to the way things were, Nathan. Give us a chance. Please. If this is about my past..."

Once upon a time, she'd been his greatest strength. Now she felt like his greatest weakness. He put the island between them. If he touched her, he'd be lost.

"This has nothing to do with your father."

Her face became stricken. "It wasn't just our past you aren't ready to face. It's Deanna, isn't it?"

Nate gripped the hard, smooth edge of the countertop. "After you broke up with me, she was my light at the end of the tunnel. I was messed up for a long time, too. Even after we got married, I kept her at an emotional arm's length. Now the guilt and love…"

"…are mixed up in your head," she rasped.

He swallowed. "Deanna's shadow will always be between us. A life with you wouldn't be fair to her."

Gemma's nostrils flared. "She's dead, Nathan, but you don't have to be."

His chest heaved. "No matter how hard we tried, we'd never work. We'd only hurt each other. Hurt the boys." Across the expanse of the granite counter, he threw her a bleak look. "I can't allow them to be hurt any more than they already have been. Don't you see?"

She opened her hands. "What I see is a man so afraid he'll be hurt, he won't allow himself to love again. Take your eyes off the past. I love you, Nathan Crenshaw. Even if you don't feel the same now, could you ever see yourself loving me in the future?"

"The last thing I want to do is hurt you." Unable to bear the anguish in her eyes, he looked away. "But the answer to your question is no. In the future I envision at the ranch, there is no you and me."

She flinched as if he'd struck her.

He clenched his jaw so hard it ached. "I will always be grateful for everything you've done for Dad. For everything you've been to Connor and Kody."

"Be honest with yourself, Nathan, if not with me." Her mouth trembled. "What has this last month been about if not falling in love?"

He forced himself to lock eyes with her. "Finishing the unfinished."

"Closure," she whispered. "Time has run out for us, hasn't it?"

"I'm sorry." He stuffed his hands in his pockets. "First loves aren't meant to be forever loves."

She wrapped her arms around herself. "I need to pack."

He frowned. "It's Christmas Day. You don't need to go now."

"You'll need time and space to prepare your father and the boys for the new caregiver. There's no point in prolonging the inevitable." She winced. "I always believed you and I were inevitable."

Once upon a time—as recently as last night—he'd thought so, too. Shattered at the prospect of her imminent departure, he wasn't sure what he believed. Only there'd be no once-upon-a-time for him and Gemma. No happily-ever-after.

He doubted he'd ever know happiness again. But this last month, he had been. Happy.

"I'll say goodbye to Ike and the boys." She edged around the island. "Then I'll go."

By the time the boys and his father returned, he'd managed to get his emotions under lock and key.

Gemma emerged with her suitcase just as he finished explaining about Mrs. Jewell.

Kody flung himself at her. "I don't want a jewel. I want Gemma."

Blinking rapidly, Connor buried his face into her side. Nate could tell it was all she could do not to burst into tears herself. But she didn't. And he was grateful.

Instead, she hugged them hard and whispered sweet, soothing words of comfort. Sensing something amiss, Rascal rubbed his coat against her leg.

His dad touched his arm. "Just because Mrs. Jewell will be here doesn't mean—"

"It's better this way, Dad," he grunted.

"Better for whom?" his father growled.

His dad drew her into a fierce, hard hug. "Thank you, dear girl. For everything you've done." He threw Nate a sad look. "For all of us."

Almost as soon as Gemma drove away, Nate wished he'd

made a different choice. But he hadn't. She was gone from his life almost as quickly as she'd reappeared.

This time, forever.

Mrs. Jewell turned out to be a pleasant, motherly sort of woman. She and Rascal took to each other right away. After reviewing the routine Gemma had created for his dad, she declared her intention to stick with it. To his credit, his father vowed to give her a fair chance.

Nate found her friendly, efficient and professional. Per the terms of their agreement, she looked after his dad, did light housekeeping and had supper on the table at the end of the day before she returned to her home near the county seat.

Everything was working out for the best. Although, the boys moped about the farmhouse like the end of the world had come. A week passed. He remained heartsick and miserable. Unable to sleep. Unable to eat.

New Year's Day came and went.

The next day, the boys returned to school. He was in the barn shoveling fresh hay into a stall when he heard the sound of an engine in the drive.

His head down, he kept working. Maybe whoever it was would go away. He wasn't in the mood for company.

A vehicle door slammed. Heavy boots clomped across the compacted snow in the barnyard toward him. He was contemplating a hasty retreat when a tall, skinny scarecrow wearing horn-rimmed glasses blocked the light between him and the door.

Worst-case scenario. Turning his back, he gripped the handle of the shovel. Great-aunt GeorgeAnne.

He was actually surprised she hadn't arrived before now. His mouth twisted. "Come to gloat?"

"I was wrong about Gemma."

He wheeled. "What happened to 'She's not from around here... She doesn't belong.'?"

GeorgeAnne pushed her glasses farther along the bridge of her nose. "Turns out she does."

"You said we weren't a good fit. We weren't a good match."

His aunt sniffed. "After I had the chance to know her, I changed my mind. Gemma would make an excellent rancher's wife. A wonderful mother to those boys of yours."

"Connor and Kody already have a mother," he growled.

She cocked her head. "That's what this fit of yours is truly about, isn't it? This has nothing to do with Gemma and everything to do with your inability to acknowledge the loss of Deanna."

"I don't need your interference in my life." He set his jaw.

She set hers. "Good. Because this isn't me interfering. This is an intervention to make sure you don't ruin your life."

He gaped at her.

"Self-pity is unattractive in anyone, much less a great, big, hulking man like yourself. Not every minute of your marriage was perfect. So what? I don't know many relationships that are. You have regrets? So do I. Congratulations. Welcome to the human race."

His jaw dropped.

"If only you'd look beyond the mistakes to the happiness you shared with Deanna. Recall the joy you gave her." Her eyes watered. "And there was so much happiness, nephew. She loved you so much. No matter how you try to deny it and shield yourself from the pain, you loved her, too. Let yourself remember. Not everyone gets a love like Deanna's. Much less two. Don't waste it. We can learn much from sorrow. I beg you, dear boy. Don't let your suffering be in vain."

"Are you finished?" His voice sounded strangled.

"I've said what I came to say."

"And then some," he muttered.

"Your father and Mrs. Jewell are headed to the Jar for an afternoon with the ROMEOs. After school, the boys are going to Maggie's. You'll have the ranch to yourself until supper." She touched his cheek. "You really are my favorite nephew, you know."

Glimpsing the compassion in her eyes, he felt his anger fade. Standing in the doorframe of the barn, he watched her drive away.

It was rare he had the farm to himself. He couldn't recall the last time he'd truly been alone for any stretch of time. Not since Gemma came into his life again.

Restless, he wandered into the house. The silence felt oppressive. Or maybe that was merely his emotions, roiling beneath the surface he kept so carefully stoic.

Seeking a distraction, he drifted into the boys' bedroom, only to be confronted with the lone picture of Deanna he'd allowed to remain. Everything else he'd packed away.

As if Deanna and what he'd felt for her could be so easily eradicated.

He picked up the framed photo of his late wife with their sons. He recalled taking the picture on an early-autumn day a few weeks before she died. She and the boys had been standing in front of one of her rose bushes.

She wasn't a pale, golden beauty like Gemma. Everything about Deanna had been bubbly and vibrant. Warm. Generous to a fault. The most loving, forgiving person he'd ever known. Or loved.

Tears sprang to his eyes. Because yes, he'd loved her. Only now could he bear to admit it to himself. He'd loved her. Deeply.

Clutching the photo to his chest, he stumbled out of the house. He found himself at the ruins of the flower garden she'd once so lovingly tended. In an effort to avoid facing the truth of his loss, the garden he'd ripped out.

But there was no bypassing sorrow. No way forward, except to go through it. His knees buckled. He sank onto the ground, paying no heed to the cold seeping through his jeans.

He'd remained dry-eyed through her funeral. Dry-eyed these last, two, bitter, lonely years without her.

One by one, memories unfolded in his mind. How beautiful she'd been on their wedding day. The joy he'd felt as she carried his sons in her belly. There'd been so much fun. So much laughter. How could he have sought to erase it?

To erase the memories would be to erase her. And that was the last thing he wanted.

Sobs overcame him. He cried out in the stillness of that January afternoon with a pain so great he wondered how it could be borne. Yet he had to bear it. Come to grips with it. So he could breathe again. Live again. Love again.

Because that's what Deanna would have wanted for him.

"I think you and Gemma would've liked each other," he whispered to the wind. "Thank you for giving me Connor and Kody. Thank you for putting me on the right path with Dad's illness."

Deanna had been first to perceive something was amiss with her father-in-law. Deanna, who insisted Nate consult a neurologist. After a ton of research, it was Deanna—he choked up—who found PawPals. And Deanna's idea to get his dad a dementia assistance dog.

Life come full circle, Deanna had set him on a path to a reunion with his first love. Deanna, who'd given him another chance at life and love. Twice...

Grief poured out of him. He mourned Deanna as he'd never allowed himself to mourn her before. "I miss you so much."

He always would. And that was as it should be. The cost of love. A price he'd pay all over again for the chance to love Deanna.

Nate turned his face to the brilliant blue of the Carolina sky.

From somewhere on the ridge, a wren was singing its heart out. His gaze landed upon something tiny and yellow poking bravely through the mantle of snow at his feet.

He brushed aside the snow. A crocus. One of Deanna's favorites. His breath hitched. In the dead of winter, she used to say, a crocus was the first harbinger that spring would come again.

Gemma might represent to him a forever summer, but Deanna would always be an eternal spring.

As a breeze dried the tears on his cheeks, peace filled him. For a second, her presence was with him so strongly he believed he might yet reach out and touch her one last time. Her love lived on in their sons. One day he and Deanna would have a reunion of their own.

But until then… He got off the ground. He loved Gemma. He wanted a life with her. Had he lost her forever? *God, what should I do?*

The glimmers of an idea etched themselves into his mind, but he would need help. He fished his phone out of his pocket. It might already be too late.

GeorgeAnne answered on the first ring as if she'd been waiting for his call. "Come to your senses yet?"

He rubbed at the kinks in his neck. "I can hardly believe I'm saying this—I need the matchmakers' help."

"I can't tell you how pleased I am the Double Name Club's new nonmeddling policy worked out so well for you." The cat-that-swallowed-the-cream glee in her voice would have been galling, if a beggar like him could've afforded to be choosy. "Better than anyone could've anticipated."

By the time his great-aunt got through rewriting history, he and Gemma would go down as yet another matchmaker triumph.

"Gemma and I were supposed to spend Christmas together. I need to make this right with her."

"Not a problem, dear boy. Ever heard of a little thing called 'The Twelve Days of Christmas'? By my reckoning, you've got about four days to fix this and still make your Christmas deadline. What are you thinking?"

"This is going to require a road trip."

GeorgeAnne chuckled. "Might be interesting to see how the flatlanders survive in their concrete jungle."

"It's Laurel Grove, Aunt Georgie. Not a concrete..." He pinched the bridge of his nose. "I'm going to need yards of chicken wire."

"On it. Your cousin Brian will haul over a bunch from the store. Next?"

"A ton of extension cords. Dozens of strands of lights, preferably white and blue."

His aunt was old school. He heard the scratching sound of pencil on paper. "What else?"

"The jeweler is closed until next week."

GeorgeAnne sniffed. "He won't be after I call him."

Suddenly overwhelmed with what it would take to pull this off, he groaned. "Who are we kidding? This will never work. Gemma may take one look at me and kick me to the curb."

"Not going to happen."

"And there's the not-so-small issue of needing a dog, Aunt Georgie."

"What kind of dog?"

He let his head drop into his hand. "What does it matter? I've got about as much chance of winning Gemma back as sprouting wings."

"Focus, nephew. What sort of qualities are you looking for in a dog for Gemma?"

"Something cute. Cuddly. And sweet. A loyal companion."

"Don't worry. Bridger has connections."

"It's going to take a lot of hands to make this happen in four days."

"Never fear, nephew. Truelove is here."

With that ominous statement, she clicked off to rally the troops. Within the hour, vehicles arrived, loaded with enthusiastic helpers and supplies. By nightfall, Nate began to believe Operation Christmas Ball—as his father dubbed it—might stand a chance of succeeding.

After everyone went home, he talked to the boys about what he hoped to do. "Would it be okay with you, guys, if Gemma came to live with us?"

Connor cocked his head. "Forever?"

"The foreverest of forever."

Connor hugged him. "Thank you, Daddy."

He gazed into their earnest little faces. "It's not a done deal, son. Gemma may not say yes."

"Of course she'll say yes, Daddy." Kody rolled his eyes. "She might be a little mad with you, but she still loves us plenty."

His dad grinned. "Out of the mouths of babes."

Whatever works... God, please. Whatever works.

Truelove was on board, but Laurel Grove reinforcements would be essential.

It was late. He'd put in a call to Juliet tomorrow. And he prayed she wouldn't hang up on him before hearing him out.

Chapter Sixteen

Alone and devastated in her apartment that week, she grieved for what had never been and what would never be with Nathan. Despite her assurances to the contrary, she had totally given in to the hope something long-term could grow between them.

Yet her initial instincts had been correct. Since that long-ago summer, too much had transpired. Their lives had followed different trajectories.

She'd hoped, prayed, that their Christmas reunion might lead to the future she'd always wanted, but she'd deluded herself.

Over the week between Christmas and New Year's, the finality of losing him—although hadn't she lost him long ago?—produced in her an ache so intense, sometimes she found it difficult to draw breath.

That first night, she'd called Juliet to let her know what had happened. Her next phone call had been to the Spencers.

Ma Spencer had wanted to cut short their Christmas vacation with the grandkids to return immediately. Gemma managed to dissuade her, but the fierce love in Ma's voice on the phone made Gemma rethink her years with them. In a state of shocked numbness following the tragedy, she'd refused to allow herself to belong to the family and home the Spencers offered.

Juliet was relentless in her repeated attempts to console.

A much-needed reminder Gemma wasn't alone. Never alone. Fifteen years ago, there'd been Juliet, the Spencers and God. In losing the love of her life, she found it to be much the same now—Juliet, the Spencers and God.

Yet knowing the outcome—that no shining future awaited her in Truelove—would she have done anything different in the last few weeks? Held back her heart? Trained Rascal for someone else?

If given the chance, she wouldn't have traded the opportunity to know Nathan's boys for anything. Or deprived Ike of what Rascal offered—a better quality of life.

As for opening her heart to Nathan?

Spending those precious weeks with him… She had no regrets for falling in love with the man he'd become. She loved Nathan. She prayed God would use their brief time together to help him move toward a new life and a new love. The boys needed a mother.

It hurt to imagine someone else mothering Connor and Kody, but Nathan deserved all the happiness in the world. It just wouldn't be with her.

A bitter, bitter truth, but it was time to move forward into the life God meant for her.

The news of her leave-taking must have quickly made the rounds of the Truelove grapevine. It meant the world that Maggie, Kara and Shayla called to check on her.

She also had time to ponder what she wanted her future to look like. It wouldn't include the boys and Nathan. But her mother's sacrifice made sure she still had a life. It was time she started living it.

On the morning of New Year's Eve, for the first time in days, she got dressed and braided her hair. Then she drove to Laurel Grove.

Gemma parked across the street from the house where her mother died. It no longer resembled the house she'd known. On that late-December day, colorful, vibrant pansies sat in pots on the front stoop. There was an air of happiness about the home of the current owners.

She wasn't entirely sure how she knew that. But for someone who'd grown up with unhappiness, it was easy to spot its opposite.

Per Shayla's sage advice, she made a deliberate choice to close that painful chapter in her past. Leaving behind her father's legacy of shame, she headed for the town cemetery.

There, she laid a bouquet of flowers at the base of her mother's headstone. She was here to embrace her mother's legacy. She was her mother's most-cherished legacy.

Gemma gazed at the milky sunshine of the cold winter's day. "Thank you, Mama. For everything."

Swiping her eyes, she returned to her car. Driving down Main Street, she steered around the back of PawPals headquarters. The office was closed for New Year's Eve, but her best friend was taking advantage of a few quiet hours to catch up on administrative tasks.

"Hey, stranger." Inside PawPals, Juliet hugged her. "I'm glad to see you out and about."

Gemma smiled, a wobbly one but a smile nonetheless. "About time, right?"

Juliet examined Gemma's features. "Grieving takes as long as it takes."

She nodded. "I've decided to give up my apartment in Greensboro. Would you help me find a new place closer to Laurel Grove?"

"You're sure about this?"

Gemma lifted her chin. "I've made my peace with the past. It's made me who I am and who I am is okay. I want to be closer to the work I love, the friends who love me and a future I've put in God's hands."

Tears sprang into Juliet's eyes.

"Put me on your apartment-hunting schedule." She draped her arm around her friend. "Would it be possible to move up the training for the next assistance dog?"

Juliet opened a file on her computer. "A black Lab. From the Hollingsworth kennel in Truelove."

"I vetted Liberty myself. Very adaptable, friendly and trainable. Who's our next client?"

Juliet clicked a few keys on the keypad. "An elderly woman near the coast. Do you want me to contact Bridger about moving up the delivery date?"

She bit her lip. "He'll bring Liberty to us, right? I won't have to—"

"You won't have to return to Truelove." Juliet moved around the desk. "I'll contact the client's family about sending the usual personal items so you can begin scent training." Her friend propped her hands on her hips. "What're your plans for tonight?"

"I plan to enjoy the Laurel Grove fireworks and celebrate the coming of the New Year with your family." Gemma's mouth twitched. "If you'll have me."

She grinned. "You're always welcome at the Melbourne house."

"Great." Gemma made a show of wiping her brow. "Because I already packed an overnight bag."

At Juliet's that night, there was fun and laughter. She got her dog fix with Sophie's sweet golden retriever, Bixby, and funny little Moose, who basically ran his humans like the alpha dog legend he was in his own doggy mind. She also spent a lot of time with baby Tyler.

She didn't know how or when, but someday she wanted children in her life. Whether that meant fostering or adoption or biological. Although, she couldn't imagine ever loving anyone like she loved Nathan. But she put the uncertainty and her hope into the hands of the One who loved her the most and the best.

God would decide if and when. And if His plan was for her to not have children, she would rest knowing He had something else in store for her. A future and a hope better than what she could imagine.

The day after New Year's, she and Juliet met for apartment hunting. They inspected two available apartments within the same complex, but during lunch, she sensed a change come over her PawPals partner.

Juliet found flaws with each of the next three places. Gemma suggested revisiting the first two, but Juliet suddenly found fault with each of them, too.

She frowned at her friend, her dark head bent over her cell phone again. Something was off. Juliet had been distracted ever since getting a phone call. There'd been a flurry of subsequent texts.

"Is everything okay, Juliet?"

Not bothering to look up from the most recent text, Juliet fluttered her hand. "Just working through some unexpected logistics. I should get home."

"I'll follow you to Laurel Grove."

"Um…" Juliet's brow creased. "Maybe you should head to Greensboro."

Gemma blinked.

"You'll need to start packing if you plan on moving out soon, right?"

"I… I guess…" She fingered the strap of her purse. "We're still on for more apartment hunting tomorrow?"

Juliet agreed, but later called and cancelled. Over the next couple of days, her friend continued to fob off Gemma's attempts to reschedule.

More than a little bummed, she reminded herself Juliet had

family and business responsibilities. She'd find her own apartment. Then just after six o'clock one evening, her cell rang.

"I think I've managed to finally pull it off," Juliet gushed.

Having not heard from her in several days, Gemma stared at the cell in her hand. "You've found me an apartment?"

"Better than that."

"A house to rent? I hadn't dared hope I could afford— You're sure it's in my budget? Room for me to train the dogs?"

"Totally within your reach, Gem. Room for lots of animals to roam around."

"Oh, Jules." She squeezed her eyes shut for a second. Juliet had been working this whole time on her behalf. "I can't thank you enough."

"Your happiness is all the thanks I ever need." Something that sounded like tears laced Juliet's voice.

"When can I—"

"First, I need you to pick up your dog."

Not her dog. A dog for their next client. Although once she moved into the house Juliet had found, maybe she'd look into acquiring her own pet.

"Oh. Okay. Sure." She frowned into the phone. "When?"

"Now."

She glanced out the window. It was already dark, and a light snowfall was expected tonight. "You want me to drive to Laurel Grove to pick up the dog now?"

"Meet me at the office. You'll head over right this minute, won't you?"

Gemma grabbed her key fob. "I'll head over this very second, I promise."

"Um...you got dressed today, didn't you?"

On her way to the door, she stopped. "Yessssss..."

"Something nice?"

Her gaze flitted to the ceiling. "I guessssss..."

Juliet's tone went brisk. "Tell me what you're wearing."

"What does it matter what I'm wearing, Jules? I'm picking up a dog, not a date."

But Juliet would not let it go until she described in detail her current attire.

"Satisfied?" she huffed. "Didn't realize there was a PawPals dress code."

"You've fixed your hair and you've put on makeup, too?"

"What's going on, Juliet?"

"Nothing."

"You're not setting me up for a blind date, are you?" she growled. "Because I'm not ready for that."

"On my 4-H camp counselor's honor, I promise a blind date is the furthest thing from my mind."

"Then if you and the fashion police are done, I'll be on my way."

"We'll be waiting."

By "we'll," she figured Juliet was counting Liberty the dog, too.

It was almost seven o'clock by the time she turned off the highway and reached Laurel Grove. Main Street storefronts lay dark and shuttered. The sidewalks rolled up at the close of the business day. She veered around the PawPals building to the employee parking lot, but there was no sign of Juliet's car.

Doing a U-turn in the empty lot, she steered into a space in front of PawPals, usually reserved for clients. No lights shone from within. Her pulse ratcheted. Where was Juliet? What was going on?

She spotted a piece of paper taped to the glass door. Switching off the engine, she retrieved the note.

Waiting on the square.

Perhaps Liberty had gotten restless and Juliet had taken her for a short walk. But in the dark?

Gemma pivoted at the same moment the square blazed to life. Whoa. At the sudden brilliance of the festive display, she threw up her hand to shield her eyes.

Similar to the larger, annual Christmas event in nearby Greensboro, dozens of blue-and-white illuminated balls hung from the bare canopy of trees dotting the square. What was with the Christmas—

Gemma checked her phone. It was January 6. Old Christmas. In some cultures celebrated as the Feast of the Three Kings. In others, Epiphany.

She'd never known Laurel Grove to celebrate Old Christmas before, but maybe it was a new tradition.

However, she didn't relish venturing into the deserted square alone. What was Juliet thinking? More than a little irritated, she sent off a quick text to her friend. There was no reply, but a pair of headlights swept across the sidewalk.

A lone vehicle pulled in beside her car. Tensing, she had her finger poised over the alarm button on her key fob when she caught sight of the man behind the wheel.

She stepped closer. "Pa?"

Getting out of the sedan she also now recognized, he drew her into a hug. "Happy Christmas, darlin'."

Her gaze darted to the lighted balls across the street. "I didn't realize Laurel Grove celebrated Twelfth Night. Is there an event planned for later?"

He chuckled. "You could say that."

Not getting the joke, she shrugged. "I didn't expect to see you for another few days."

"Juliet called. We came home early to meet your new dog."

"You drove from Virginia to meet my latest K-9?"

He grinned. "Ma thought you might need a little last-minute reassurance so she sent me over to encourage you."

"I don't understand."

He put his arm around her shoulder. "To tell you how proud your mother would be of the young woman you've become."

Tears stung her eyes. "Whatever I've become is because you and Ma made me feel safe enough to follow my dreams."

"And now you have another dream to follow." Releasing her, he gestured in the direction of the square. "You better head over before we're frozen."

She bit her lip. "You'll go with me?"

"Not this time, darlin'." He leaned against his car. "But I'll be here when you come back. Like always."

Her gaze cut to the illuminated globes across the street.

"Go on now." Pa Spencer gave her a little push. "You've waited long enough."

She looked at him.

"Don't be afraid." He smiled. "All will come right in the end. At long last, just like I told you."

Once upon a terrible, terrible day, he'd made her that promise.

Gentle snowflakes floated down around them. Reminding her of a first snowfall under the dark Truelove sky with Nathan. And his kiss. A memory, no matter how things turned out, she would cherish forever.

She crossed the street. The snow crunched under her boots. It was only after she stepped into the grove of trees it occurred to her to wonder how Pa knew Juliet's note had told her to meet in the square. But by then, it was too late to turn around and ask.

The glittering panorama of Christmas balls enveloped her. It was as if everything outside the square had ceased to exist. She found herself in a world of its own. A beautiful world.

No sign of Juliet, but on the path leading to the center of the square sat a small wicker basket. Something wiggled underneath the warm, fuzzy blue blanket lining the basket.

There was a whimper. She put her hand to her throat. A tiny

black nose peeked out from the blanket. Two round black eyes like buttons peered out at her. The fluffy, white, powder-puff Maltese puppy cocked his head at her and barked.

Relaxing, she smiled. "Hello, you." Crouching, she let the dog smell her hand. "Have you gotten yourself lost?"

The puppy licked her fingers.

Unable to resist, she plucked the dog from the basket and cuddled him—it was a him—close to her coat. "Where's your human, sweet little pup?"

There was a tag on the Maltese's collar. Winston. Only Jules had known Gemma's favorite dog name. Her breath caught. And Nathan.

A note was attached to his collar. "Will you keep me for-ever?"

Jules and her little jokes. Whoever this dog belonged to, it wasn't her. The adorable puppy wasn't the black Labrador she was expecting from Bridger, either. But Winston would make someone a wonderful companion pet.

Finding a leash coiled in the basket, she clipped it onto Winston's collar. Best not to get too attached. She'd said the same when she went to Truelove. And look how well that turned out.

Maybe Juliet had also taken it upon herself to gift Gemma with a pet of her own. She set Winston on his feet. His nose twitching, he yanked Gemma forward. A small dog but mighty in heart. His paws scrabbling in the fresh-fallen snow, he uncovered something and promptly ate it.

"Winston! No. Don't eat—"

He yanked her forward. He pounced again, but this time she beat him to it. Someone had left a trail of dog treats for Winston to follow. What further surprises lay in store?

Smiling, she decided to play along. What a lovely gesture. Jules's latest effort to lift her spirits. What a good best friend she was.

For such a little dog, Winston set a fast pace. She emerged

in the center of the square fully expecting to find her best friend and possibly Sophie, Tyler and Rob.

But what she discovered was better. So much better. Encircled by an enormous heart of rose petals, crimson against the snow, stood Nathan, handsome in his Sunday Stetson, a suit and a tie.

She ground to an immediate halt. "What are you doing here?" she whispered, hardly able to believe her eyes. "Has something happened to the boys? To Ike?"

"Everyone is fine." He cleared his throat. "Except for me."

She scooped Winston into her arms. "What's wrong?"

"Nothing's been the same since you left." He scrubbed his hand over his face. "Many, many people have taken care to point out my stubborn pigheadedness."

"Comparing yourself to a pig...that seems terribly unfair." She cut her eyes at him. "To the pig."

His mouth twitched. "I can't begin to tell you how much I've missed you, Gemma Spencer."

She tilted her head. "Try."

"Why don't you step into the heart with me and I'll try to explain?"

She narrowed her eyes at him. "I can hear you fine from here. Why don't you start by explaining what you're doing in Laurel Grove."

"You leave me no choice, except to use every tool at my disposal."

He whipped out a squeaky rubber duck. Winston lunged. Trying to maintain her grip on the small dog, she stumbled into the petal-strewed heart.

"No fair, Nathan Crenshaw." She glowered at him. "Using the dog against me."

Seizing the duck between his jaws, the Maltese shook his head from side to side, chomping down. Rolling her eyes, she set Winston on his feet, but kept a tight hold on the leash and her wildly careening emotions.

"That's better." Nathan smiled. "I'm here to apologize for the things I said. I also believed it high time you had a dog of your own."

Her mouth opened. "Winston's for me?"

"You told Dad the way to your heart was through a dog."

Her eyes widened. "All of this…" She motioned. "It's about giving me a pet?"

"All of this took the combined efforts of a lot of people who care about you. I've had half of Truelove making Christmas balls to my exact specifications. And half of Laurel Grove, including the Spencers, Juliet and the Knit-Knack Club working this end on your behalf."

She shook her head. "It's kind of you to think of me—"

"I haven't been able to stop thinking about you, Gemma," he grunted.

Her lips trembled. "First loves are never meant to be forever loves. Isn't that what you said? Is Winston supposed to be a consolation prize?"

"This isn't going the way I…" He pinched the bridge of his nose. "When you asked me if I could ever see my way to loving you—"

"You said you couldn't."

"I lied." His Adam's apple bobbed in his throat. "But I promise I'll never lie to you again." His gaze bored into hers. "You're all I see. I can't imagine a future without you. Loving Connor and Kody. Loving me," he rasped. "Unless…" He looked away.

"Unless what?"

His gaze found hers. "Unless you don't love me anymore. I wouldn't blame you if you didn't."

The aching vulnerability on his face nearly buckled her knees.

"I do love you." She shut her eyes and opened them. "I always have."

"Then ask me your question again." He took her hands in his. Tingles from the always-something-between-them flew up her arm. She could tell from the wry twist of his lips he felt it, too.

"Sparks have never been our problem," she whispered. "That summer—"

"This is so not about a long-ago summer." He locked eyes with her. "Please, Gemma. Ask me again how I feel about you."

"What about Deanna?"

"There will always be a place in my heart that belongs to her. She's the mother of my sons." A muscle throbbed in his cheek. "But tonight, there's no one here but you and me."

"And Winston."

Nathan smiled at the Maltese sitting at their feet.

Pa Spencer had been right. She'd waited long enough for the man standing in front of her. She would wait no more.

"Do you love me, Nathan?"

His face gentled. "From the moment you stepped out of the shadow of the barn your first day at the ranch... One glance and you had my heart. Again. I love you, Gemma. I doubted seventeen-year-olds could experience true love. In our case, it turns out they can."

She made no effort to stem the flow of tears down her cheeks. He pulled a ring from his coat pocket and dropped to his knee.

Gasping, she put her hand to her mouth. Was this really happening? Or merely a dream?

But at the warm touch of his strong hand taking hers, she knew it was for real. God's plan for her. The future she'd longed for.

"Will you share all my tomorrows?" His voice went husky. "Will you marry me?"

"Yes." She quivered. "I will."

With a whoop, he jumped to his feet and pressed his mouth against hers. Clasped in his arms, he swung her around.

In a frenzy of doggy delirium, Winston raced back and forth across the rose-encircled heart, scattering crimson petals to the wind.

Cradling his face between her hands, she smiled against his lips. "We've got Winston's approval."

He grinned. "Rascal can't wait for the pup to join the High Country Ranch on a permanent basis."

She cocked her head. "Rascal's met Winston?"

"The boys, too. Who do you think scent-trained him to follow the treats?"

"Your dad is okay about us?"

"Sweetheart..." Nathan shook his head. "Dad's been after me to pop the question since the week you arrived."

"It takes some people a little longer than others to clue in, I guess," she teased.

His arms tightened around her. "I got here eventually. Where I was always meant to be."

"Me, too." She brushed her mouth across the rough stubble on his jaw. "All's well that ends well."

Closure. Life come to its full, glorious circle. Happily-ever-after.

"There's plenty of room at your new home for K-9 training."

Home. She smiled, thinking of Juliet's phone call. Room for all kinds of animals, she'd said. *Thank You, God. And thank you, Juliet, for putting the pieces of this magical night together.*

"When will you make me the happiest man on earth?"

She laced her fingers around the nape of his neck. "As soon as we're reunited with the family."

Her own family to love and cherish.

Nathan cocked his head. "The boys and Dad are at Juliet's. 'Scared to death,' to quote Kody, I'll mess this up for him."

She pressed her forehead against his. "I don't need anything fancy. Just you. And the boys."

Barking, Winston continued to race around them.

Nathan lifted his head. "Can somebody come get this dog and give us a moment?" he hollered.

"Who are you talking—"

A sheepish grin lightening his rugged features, Bridger sauntered out of the trees. Securing the leash, he touched his hand to his forehead in a brief salute before heading off again.

"We've had witnesses?"

"The half of Truelove I mentioned before? Yeah. The matchmakers, too."

She gaped at him.

"At a discreet distance, I assure you. Reinforcements in the event of dire disaster. Like you throwing the ring in my face."

"Marry me tomorrow," she breathed.

Through the opening in his coat, she felt his heartbeat kick up a notch. "I'm yours forever, Gemma Spencer, but how do you aim to pull this off tomorrow?"

"Laurel Grove's got churches." She smiled. "When the Double Name Club of Truelove combines forces with the Knit-Knack Club of Laurel Grove, there's not much those ladies can't accomplish."

"Possibly even world domination," he joked.

First loves could be forever loves. The best of loves. They'd waited long enough for their happily-ever-after.

His eyes shone. "The best is yet to be, sweetheart."

"Kiss me," she whispered.

Sweeping her off her feet, he did.

* * * * *

Dear Reader,

I hope you enjoyed Gemma and Nathan's heartfelt, painstaking journey to true love.

My heart goes out to those who walk or have walked alongside a loved one struggling with dementia. It is a long goodbye. A thousand little deaths. Losing them one inch at a time. This was a hard book for me to write. It brought back a lot of painful memories from my father's battle with Alzheimer's. He loved dogs. I wished there'd been a Rascal for him during his illness. But God's grace was sufficient for him. And for me. Providing strength to make hard decisions. To persevere despite the grief during what unfolded. God's blessing to me that even at the end, my dad still knew who I was. In 2016, he went Home.

It is through Christ, we find our forever Home—the true Happily-Ever-After for which we were created. Thank you for telling your friends how much you enjoy the Truelove matchmaker series.

I'd love to connect with you. You can contact me at lisa@lisacarterauthor.com or visit lisacarterauthor.com, where you can also subscribe to my author newsletter for news about upcoming book releases and sales.

In His Love,
Lisa Carter